THE ONE: FALLING IN LOVE FOREVER ANTHOLOGY

THE ONE: FALLING IN LOVE FOREVER ANTHOLOGY

SAPPHIRE BOOKS

SALINAS, CALIFORNIA

The One: Falling in Love Forever Anthology
Copyright © 2016. All rights reserved.

ISBN - 978-1-943353-31-6

This is a work of fiction - names, characters, places, and incidents are the product of the author's imagination or are used fictitiously. Any resemblance to actual persons living or dead, business, events or locales is entirely coincidental.

All rights reserved. No part of this publication may be reproduced, distributed, or transmitted in any form or by any means, including photocopying, recording, or other electronic or mechanical methods, without written permission of the publisher.

Editor - Elizabeth M. Hodge
Book Designer - LJ Reynolds
Cover Designer - Michelle Brodeur

Sapphire Books Publishing, LLC
P.O. Box 8142
Salinas, CA 93912
www.sapphirebooks.com

Printed in the United States of America
First Edition – April 2016

This and other Sapphire Books titles can be found at
www.sapphirebooks.com

Acknowledgements

This anthology springs from the romantic women of Sapphire Books and all the wonderful contributors who entrusted their stories to us.

"She is a friend of mind. She gather me, man. The pieces I am, she gather them and give them back to me in all the right order. It's good, you know, when you got a woman who is a friend of your mind."

Toni Morrison

Soul meets soul on lovers' lips.

Percy Bysshe Shelley

Table of Contents

Preface

If lucky enough, we fall in love once in a lifetime. In a way, the discovery of the person meant for us, the being with whom our soul becomes mated seems promised to us. Children's books and romance novels promise an encounter with a beautiful, mythical love – a passionate lover that sweeps us off kilter and changes everyday life into happily-ever-after. Indeed, most expect to find a soul mate; although, many find that the storybook romance never quite pans out.

In reality, most fall in love a couple of times throughout a lifetime. Yet, those relationships fail to fulfill the "forever" expectancy – they end. Still, we hope that love, true and eternal, will embrace us. We hope that stardust will cover the banal when life becomes monotonous or loneliness grasps us too firmly when days fades to night. Never give up hope. True love, one that emanates between two joined hearts exists. Typically, it finds us later in life, when least expected, and when both parties find their hearts ready to receive it.

Everyone deserves happily ever after!
Elizabeth M. Hodge

The Cost of Love

Beth Burnett

Sarah leaned back against the window frame, hoping the slight night breeze would offer some relief. A bead of sweat slid down her neck continuing between her breasts. Across the room, Lacey followed its path with her eyes before it disappeared into the waistband of Sarah's boxers.

"Sultry," Sarah mumbled. "Isn't that what you call it?"

Lacey smiled. "The sultry summer heat."

Sarah rolled her eyes, lazily fanning herself with the paper she had folded into a makeshift fan. "I've never understood what you see in this place."

Sighing, Lacey stretched, running a hand across her wet forehead. She pushed back the limp strands of hair that were hanging in her face. Maybe it was time to consider shaving it all off the way Sarah had. She glanced across the room, admiring the smooth roundness of her wife's head.

Sarah caught her look and smiled, shaking her head. She reached up to brush her own fuzzy head. "I guess I could have made more of an effort to fit in."

Lacey stood, stretching her arms into the air. She waved her fingers over her head before folding into a forward bend. Her back cracked slightly as she hung face down over her feet. "Who needs a studio for hot yoga?"

Sarah laughed. She stood and crossed the room to Lacey, her long legs making the journey in three steps. Lacey unfolded to a standing position. Looking up into Sarah's face, she tried to smile but she couldn't make the corners of her mouth turn up. She blinked against impending tears.

Sarah wrapped her arms around her wife, enfolding the smaller woman into her strong arms. "I hate that I've brought this on you," she whispered.

Lacey shook her head against Sarah's shoulder. "It wasn't you. It's not you. It's this fucking town. This redneck mentality."

The women separated and Sarah moved back to the window. She looked down on the quiet street. The chirping crickets and the gentle humming sound of the fan in the next-door neighbor's window were the only immediate sounds. If she strained her ears, at the very edge of her reach, Sarah thought she could hear the stirring of the wind in the trees. She leaned further out, getting no relief in the hot air. Perhaps she was imaging the sound. She leaned out as far as she could, holding onto the frame for support. In the shadows cast by a neighbor's front light, she could just see the bumper of Lacey's car in the driveway. She leaned even further, looking at the body of the vehicle. Sarah had spent hours scrubbing the spray paint, the end result being that most of the original paint was ruined and the faint outline of "dyke" was still visible on the driver's side door. Not from here, though. From here, it just looked like a regular Ford Focus. She turned away from the window.

"I should have been there," she exclaimed suddenly, making Lacey jump. "I should have been there."

Lacey shrugged. "It wasn't your fault. They were

asshole teenagers making fools of themselves."

"Fools?" Sarah tugged on the short spikes of her buzz cut. "Fools? They weren't fools, Lace. They were and are dangerous criminals who could have killed you."

"They didn't mean to go that far."

Sarah curled her fingers into tight fists and clutched them against her chest. "They hurt you! They painted slurs on your car. How can you treat this so lightly?"

Lacey looked down at the floor. She spread her hands out helplessly. "I have no other way to treat it. I've lived in this town my entire life. I know those boys' parents. Amos Dandy's mom and I were cheerleaders together. Hell, I made out with her once behind the bleachers at a game."

"And that somehow makes this all right? They attacked you. And you aren't even going to press charges?"

"How can I do that? How can I ruin everyone's lives over an act of vandalism?"

"Vandalism? Lacey, they're monsters."

Sighing, Lacey shook her head. She crossed to the window Sarah had vacated. Picking up the discarded paper fan, she waved it at her face, stirring up some air. "Why is it so fucking hot in this house?"

Sarah sat on the edge of the bed. The humid air and the high heat were making her crazy. She tapped her fingers on the side of the mattress, staring at her wife.

Lacey looked back from the window. "Maybe it's time to invest in central air in this old place."

"It's time to sell it and move somewhere more progressive," Sarah replied. "Somewhere I don't have to worry about my wife being attacked for being my wife."

"Babe, it was an isolated incident."

"Is that what you want to call it?" Sarah slapped her hand down on the side of the bed. "I call it the redneck mentality making these little assholes think they have a right to judge you." She paused. "Us."

Lacey leaned out the window as Sarah had a few minutes before. She caught a glimpse of the bumper of her car. She knew she couldn't get as much of a view as her wife did. At five foot six she sometimes felt dwarfed by her long, lanky lover. She glanced back at Sarah, smiling. "I'm not saying it's okay. I need you to understand that. I'm not saying that what they did was okay. They spray painted my car and when I caught them doing it, they shoved me out of the way and took off. I fell. I got hurt. It sucks. It could have been worse."

Sarah stood suddenly, raising her arms to her head. She paced toward Lacey and back to the bed. "That's exactly it, Lacey! That's exactly what I'm talking about. It could have been worse. If this were even the only thing, maybe it would be easier to forgive. But the mailbox, the random yelled comments, the way Mr. Frisch glares at me whenever I buy groceries. I'm sick of being the token dykes in this town. I'm sick of it. What's going to happen next? Next time you might not just fall. Next time, they might kill you."

Lacey looked at the ground. When she looked up, she had tears in her eyes. "This is my home. My career. My family. My nieces. My everything. Are you asking me to leave all of this? Where would we go? You weren't happy where you were before."

Sarah shook her head. "I don't know. We can find a place. A place for lesbians." She paused, chuckling. "A magical place filled with Ferron concerts and unicorns."

Lacey walked slowly toward Sarah. She wrapped her arms around Sarah's waist, looking up at her with teary eyes. Sarah pulled Lacey in close.

The two women breathed together, holding tight until their heart beats found the same rhythm. Leaning back just slightly, Lacey kissed the tip of Sarah's chin. "What would you have me do, baby?"

Silent, Sarah thought about it. She didn't love this small, southern town, but she did love Lacey. After years in the city, lonely years of dating without feeling, one night stands without connection, she finally found her heart in the form of this tiny firecracker with long hair and a southern accent. There would always be problems, whether it came in the form of local hoodlums or the day-to-day challenges of a lifelong relationship. In the end, all that mattered was this woman in her arms.

Sarah bent her neck so she could reach Lacey's mouth with hers. "I don't want you to die for me. Not now, not ever."

Lacey smiled. "I'm not going to die. But, sweet one, if I were to die, dying for love would be the only reason to do it."

Beth Burnett is the award-winning author of three novels through Sapphire Books Publishing. Her passion in life is empowering other women and to that end, she teaches online self-love classes. She runs the GCLS writing academy and sits on the board as a Director of Membership. In her spare time, she is pursuing her MA in Creative Writing, working on her fourth novel, and trying to perfect the ultimate invention that would keep her cat off of the keyboard.

Love, Conversationally
Elizabeth Hodge

When I fall in love, it will be forever..."
Works in song lyrics—**Not for emotionally repressed women who chose to identify with cyborgs.** My life consists of serial relationships, built upon the momentary lust that morphed into love of a sort—adequate, comfortable, but unfulfilling. If I ignore the sad truth that I am unhappy, then perhaps accepting tolerable will suffice. Unfortunately, I cannot ignore the loneliness. Funny, how I can be lonely while sitting in the same room as my partner. Oh well.

Perhaps I am jaded, but I am put off a bit by plot lines that insist upon soul mates as beings who "complete" you or by "love" as the phenomenon that completes you. Rubbish, as all together illogical. If things end, and they do, the logically one becomes half, and half a person isn't a person at all. Why can't a woman be stronger, or complemented by the other person, and still be able to exist, to thrive alone – complete in her own skin regardless? It seems to be the case that writers assume the necessity of coupling in order for a person to become a fully formed entity. I disagree. Furthermore, I don't think that a soul mate need be a lover. Why not a soul mate as the friend that is has always been in one's life, regardless of circumstances?

Honestly, I'm not interested in a happily ever after, because the "ever after' is a continuum. Like everything life is shifting, changing, emerging. Even when outcomes appear determined, the possibility that an element comes to the fore to shift the path comes around. Perhaps it's my philosophical, essentially jaded disposition coloring this perspective. Romance is naught but angst in waiting.

True love announced her presence, quietly, conversationally, on Tuesday evening. Listening to a voice as familiar as her own, Liz felt *ennui* slip away completely. The realization that "The One," love forever after, was her dearest friend made her laugh. Perhaps she should trust that the whispers instinct told her hard intellectual head were inevitably true.

When love entered, the self-deception rapt in years of journal entries and intellectual conversations about the contrivance of happy endings fell away. Liz long accepted an ordinary, familiar life, because of simplicity, and conventionality. People are supposed to marry, couple, live as two – even when living with the other person felt stifling, right? When Liz decided that she had to find authenticity in life, she found the woman who shifted her prose to poetry, anguish to joy.

Attempting to render the accuracy of love conventionally, in words, tends to miss the mark, skittering into trite or falling into the goo. How can one convey the intensity of an emotion that exists beyond words? Love inhabits the skin, a visceral presence that announces itself despite any attempts to quell it. When you're in love, there's no escaping it and definitely, no way to hide it. For this writer, prose became poetry. Hopefully not cheesy poetry!

Visceral Love

What would the rules be if we touched?
Would friendship continue in the morning?
Or would sex destroy everything?
But…
If we touched
Sex would be the last thing on my mind.
Love
Emotion made flesh
Would overwhelm me
My body
Reacting to your presence
Would remember
Why my skin
Becomes electrified every time I see you
My hands would slide down your arms
So I could grab your hands
And entwine my fingers with yours
And just look into your eyes
Facing you
Asking your permission
To continue
To show you how much I want you
Now
Like I have for so long
As I want to for as long as you'll let me
If
If then,
My lips will softly glide across yours
And my body will move in closer
Until I know that you want
What I know that I do
And then

Only then
Will I press harder against you
Kiss with meaning
Promising more
Start to show you how much more
I am willing to give you
At that moment
And for so many more moments
Hands that will pull you closer
Circling your back
Play with the fabric of your jeans
Slide up and down, drawing patterns
Creating a tapestry
Of clothes to be shed
And sheets that need to be tangled
As I ease you down
Never releasing you
Ever kissing you
Climbing atop you
Always looking into your eyes
Knowing that I must see you
To make sure that this isn't a dream
This is real
And that what I'm feeling
The heat
The need
For you to be inside of me
As I am inside of you
Will be more than the rhythm
More than the flow of the wetness that I feel
From both of us
More than the arching
And reaching
More than the sighing

And crying out
But the completeness
Of love
Making love
Creating a union of flesh
That's just makes the love that I feel
Known to you
Real to both of us
Not a destruction of a friendship
But the creation of us
A pairing
A mating
A union
Of two
Friends
Seeking everything
Finding love
Making
Rules of touching

Souls

So I retract my previous statement: I believe in soul mates and love ever after. I found her. I found love, conversationally.

Elizabeth M. Hodge, author of the award winning poetry collection, Undone. If asked, she would describe herself as a geeky, nerdy sort of person who enjoys living in the moment.

Dear Esperanza

Tammy Bird

Raleigh, North Carolina, 2015

Thirty-one-year-old Jasmine sat on the balcony of her third floor apartment and looked out at the common area where early morning risers were milling about. It was a chilly March morning, her favorite. She sat in her black iron rocker curled in a blanket with a dog-eared dictionary and a leather-bound journal in her lap, contemplating her life. Her mom had taught her a game years ago that she still played today. "Close your eyes, Jasmine. Open to a random page. Three times. Those are your words for the day. Get that brain moving, mami. Work them into your entry." She looked down at the blank page and reached for the dictionary. *Okay, mom. Let's see what we get.* She flipped open the dictionary, eyes closed, and pointed. *Final. Hmmmmm. Okay. Final.* She repeated the ritual twice more. *Precipice. Struggle.* She looked back toward the brightening sky contemplating how she was going to use this trio of words in today's entry. She let the memory of her past mix with sounds drifting quietly through the cracked opening in the patio door behind her.

> *Mom,*
> *Life is strange. Nothing, I have learned, is final. For years I stood on the edge of a precipice that offered*

the beauty of darkness and peace. I wanted desperately to free-fall, to stop feeling. Today I stand on the edge of a different abyss – parenthood. Today I struggle not with loss or death, but with birth and the enormous duty that comes with being responsible for a life unlived. I am terrified.

Tears were rolling down Jasmine's cheeks. She stopped writing and wiped her cheeks with the sleeve of her sweatshirt.

Outer Banks, North Carolina, 2000

Two women glided side by side across the lawn that separated the neighboring houses, in perfect sync, as if choreographed. A beautiful duo with short sandy hair, they exuded confidence and energy, and Jasmine's young body took notice in a way that made her both uneasy and excited. She heard her mom in her head. *It is just part of growing up, Jasmine.*

She had been thirteen at the time, and had told her mom that she wanted to marry Crystal Moore. "But boys are hairy and they don't make me laugh," she had countered, still not understanding the finality of what her mom had said.

Her mom had been silent then, but the look on her face was one Jasmine would never forget. Anger. Jasmine had never spoken again of that day or of any feelings that she had toward any female. *Shit,* she thought, turning her face up toward the two women who had just mounted the last step of beach house's wrap around porch. *It is too early in the frigging morning for this shit.*

"I am Veronica Montgomery," the taller, tanner, bustier woman said, nodding to her right. "And this is my daughter, Ana Grace Montgomery."

"I'm Jasmine Esperanza Castillo-Brookes." Jasmine looked at Mrs. Montgomery and then toward her father. "And this is my father, Martin Brookes."

"What kind of name is Esperanza," Ana said and grinned. "How'd you get a middle name like Esperanza?"

"Ana Grace," Ana's mother scolded. "Use your manners."

Jasmine looked at Ana's face, avoiding those light denim blue eyes that she knew would suck her in, and replied with what disparagement she could muster, "My mother's Spanish heritage slammed smack into my father's Anglo-Saxton heritage, that's how.

Ana was not fazed by Jasmine's scorn. She looked her new neighbor up and down, as if she was taking inventory: Dodger's hat, dark chocolate eyes behind stylish black rimmed glasses, and a scowl that wasn't quite convincing. Slender and strong, boyishly beautiful. "Well, Jasmine Esperanza, I like you."

≈≈≈≈

That night, Jasmine sat cross-legged in the middle of her bed and touched three random words in the dictionary: *in; ever; lavender.*

Mom,

Today, Ana Grace moved in next door. I can't stop thinking about the way she looked at me. She smelled so good, like lavender and vanilla. I know I shouldn't, but I want to kiss her, stand forehead to forehead and whisper to her. I know you think it is wrong, mom, but I don't think I am going to outgrow this. Ever.

Jasmine swallowed hard. Should she rip the page out? No. These were her thoughts, her words. She took a deep breath and closed the book.

Raleigh, North Carolina, 2015

Jasmine was an emotional wreck. Her wife was having a baby today. They were having a baby today. She still fought feelings of inadequacy, of impending doom. The difference between her sixteen-year-old self and her thirty-one-year-old self, however, was that now she fought. And – for the most part – she won. Life in Raleigh was good. Her job at the mariner's museum was good. And now she was going to be a mom, which was very, very good. She dabbed once more at her eyes and turned back to her journal entry.

I can still see the day you died, mom. It was pouring down rain, cold. And I can still hear the words of the police officer: "He was on his cell phone, crossed the solid yellow line…She died instantly." The truth is, mom, I used to blame you. You left me and pop. I hated you for that.

She stopped writing again when the tears made the page swell where they landed. She had never let those words slide onto the page before, though they had always been right below the surface. Her own journey into motherhood was forcing her to face, accept, and let go. She listened for movement in the house. "Okay in there?"

"Yes, my Jazzy love, all is well. I will let you know when it is time."

Her wife's voice was surprisingly calm for a woman who would soon give birth to their first child.

They had decided to have a home birth after doing their tour at the hospital.

"It's too sterile, Jazz. I don't want our baby born into this environment," her wife had said.

"Then where?"

"Home."

"Home? What the…?"

"With a midwife."

The thought of being away from the technologies of the hospital freaked Jasmine the fuck out, but she would do anything to make her wife happy. And so it was. Helen came with impressive credentials, and she had impressed both girls from their first meeting with her kindness and knowledge. They had decided that there would be no one else present. Jasmine had no one, and Ana's family could come after. She heard the two women talking in the house. Helen had arrived at five. It was now seven. Contractions were getting closer, but dilation was still minimal. Jasmine had been called a worry wart and sent out of the house after continually inquiring about timing.

"She or he will come when ready, Jasmine," Helen had chastised softly. "You must find something to do to calm your nerves while we wait. You are not helping."

Jasmine had opted to come out here, to sit in the sun until she was needed inside. The sun felt good on her body. She wished her mom was here. She wished her dad was here. But she had wished both of those things a million times. Neither would ever come true.

Outer Banks, North Carolina, 2007

Jasmine's love of books and isolation came honestly. She and her mother had read and written together since she could hold a pencil. A journalist who had studied many long and laborious hours to learn English before coming to this country, Rosario had better written and spoken grammatical skills than anyone Jasmine had ever met. Her father, Martin, was quiet by nature. The blonde-haired, green-eyed carpenter, who was as loyal as he was handsome, spent hours honing his craft. He had built the house they now lived in as well as many along the islands. He once told Jasmine that loving her and her mom was a calling. *Yes,* Jasmine thought as she remembered. *You were a man with strong hands, kind eyes, and a loyal heart, Pops, and I adored you.*

When Rosario died, Martin had gotten smaller, his hands shook, and his eyes became bloodshot holes of murky pain. He and Jasmine quit laughing, quit talking. Each wanted to die. Only one wanted also to live.

Jasmine was twenty-three with a brand new bachelor's degree in geology and an offer to intern at a marine science museum in Raleigh. She hoped the move would give her strength to stop grieving, to stop fearing what she couldn't control. She dreaded leaving her dad, but she knew it was the only way out of the hell they had created in memory of her mom.

❧❧❧❧

It was a Wednesday, and two things happened on Wednesday. Jasmine met Ana for breakfast and coffee at Buxton's *Cup of Inspiration*, and the cleaning crew let themselves in to clean from 11:00 to 1:00. Looking back on that day, Jasmine knew her dad planned that morning based on this information. She knew he would not have wanted her to be the one to find him hanging from a wood beam in the workshop, knew that he had been so intent on his plan that he did not hear the car pull back into the driveway or the footsteps across the kitchen floor. Jasmine pictured the moments before she entered the garage. The likely scenario played over and over again in her head. Her dad, lifting his foot to kick the chair out from under himself, realizing what was happening, hearing his daughter calling to him. "Pops? Where are you? I forgot my wallet. I'll see you…" His foot making contact with the chair as he realized she was coming through the doorway, down the two steps into the workshop. She could hear his thoughts in her own head, "No. No. This was not how it was supposed to happen." And then, for both of them, the world went dark.

❧ ❧ ❧ ❧

Jasmine screamed. The chair crashed to the ground. Her father's body jerked against the rope. She had never heard such a strange mix of sounds. For a moment everything seemed to be moving in slow motion. Her hands reaching for the chair, trying to get her father's legs back on solid ground, trying to hold him up enough to stop the rope from strangling the last bit of air from his body. Looking up at the rafter, across to the assembly table, and back to the rope. At least three feet of space. Too much to cross without letting her father go. *Think Jasmine. Think.* Somehow she managed to think clearly enough to remember the wire cutters in the workbench drawer. Cut the rope. Lower the body. Check for breathing. Dial 911. Report what you know. "My father hung himself. Yes. He is still breathing. Barely. His workshop. Exposed rafters.

Yes. Still breathing."

Jasmine looked around. The smell of freshly cut wood and the sounds of the drills and saws had made this such a magical place in her years of youthful innocence, before her mom died. Before she hated them both for abandoning her. *Look around mom. How about that charm you thought the rafters added against the cement of the walls and floor.* She looked around the space, smelled the rotting untouched wood in the bins and disintegrating leather from a dilapidated old chair, almost choked from the scents mingling with the sickly smell of sweat, and the sounds of soft gurgles coming from her father's throat. The operator stayed on the line. They both heard the sirens at the same moment.

"Stay with me, Jasmine. They are almost there."

In the ambulance, Jasmine felt every beep of the monitors that signaled another breath. And then they stopped. And her father was dead.

Raleigh, North Carolina, 2015

"Jasmine," Helen called from the house. "It's time."

Jasmine shook off the thoughts of death and sadness. She had so much to be thankful for today. The love of her life was just inside that door. Together they were going to bring a son or daughter into the world. "Coming."

"Hey you," Ana said as Jasmine approached her side.

"Hey back, little momma. How's the bean?"

"Ready."

Jasmine grinned.

They still didn't know the sex of their unborn child. "Seems to me that the announcement at the moment of birth is a big part of the excitement," Jasmine had said when they talked about it. They also had no name picked out, though they had talked about many.

Helen stood at the end of the bed. "Let's take a look. Jasmine, would you like to see?"

Jasmine waited for the contraction to stop so her wife would release her hand, and moved toward the spot where Helen stood. There were no words for the love and awe that she felt. "The head. Hair. Black hair." She couldn't find the words. Chills ran through her body. They had chosen a donor of Spanish decent to match Jasmine's background, so the color was no surprise; however, the sheer all-encompassing love that she felt for this unborn child, was. Jasmine could not remember ever feeling this much for another human being.

Things moved quickly, then. More contractions. Yelling. Crying. Pushing. Again and again. Jasmine was scared. So scared. And excited. She moved from the head of the bed to the foot, wanting to be both places at once. And then *she* was here. "It's a girl," Helen said. "It's a girl," Jasmine repeated. "A beautiful little girl." The cries from the newest Castillo-Brookes filled the room. Helen helped Jasmine cut the cord and placed the baby in her arms.

An hour later, Helen took the newest little one away to to measure and clean. Jasmine sat still next to her dozing wife, her mother and father creeping back into her thoughts in the quiet room.

Outer Banks, North Carolina, 2007

Jasmine glanced at her phone to check the time as she struggled to wake herself from another restless night of dreams. Her mom, bloody, begging her to come with her, her dad, laughing as he dangled from the homemade noose in his closet, and Ana, telling her over and over again that she was a freak, a weirdo stuck in the past who would never be loved. Her father had been dead for several weeks. Each day brought new pain. She rubbed her eyes and reached for her journal and, out of habit, her dictionary. *Choice.* Again. *Cacophony.* And again. *People.* She thought about the combination for a moment.

> *Mom,*
> *You have dad. The choices the two of you made left me with no real family. I am alone, dead inside. Fuck the cacophony of wails, cackles and moans inside my head. Fuck living. Fuck dead people.*

She thought about the rafter and the sound her father's neck had made as it snapped. *I could do it. It would be quick.* Before the thought swelled, her phone buzzed against the wood of the nightstand. Ana's picture pulsated. "Fuck you," she hissed at the screen, wishing she was strong enough to ignore the hum. She swiped the screen. "Hey."

"Hey yourself. I thought I would come by for a few. I'm actually almost there."

"Sure. I'm jumping in the shower."

"See you in twenty."

Jasmine watched Ana's picture disappear. She looked at the black screen. "And fuck you and your girlfriend always trying to sound so chipper."

Ana and Marla had come by to check on her over the last few weeks. She knew that it wasn't Marla's favorite thing to do. Jasmine wasn't her favorite person, hadn't been since Marla and Ana started dating a year ago and Ana thought it was a good idea to confess to Marla her love for Jasmine.

"Why in the fuck did you do that?" Jasmine had asked her when Ana told her about the fight she and Marla had shortly after they began dating.

"She asked. I wasn't going to lie. I also told her that you were a little ho bag who fucked everything that walked – except me."

"Well, there's that."

"Fuck you."

"No."

"I hate you."

"I know. I hate you, too. I'm still not going to fuck you, though."

❧❧❧❧

Ana pushed open the front door and walked to the back of the house. She and Jasmine had spent so many hours here, laughing, crying, fighting, dreaming. Some days she wished they could go back. Adulting sucked most days, like today, when she had already spent several hours fighting with the girl that she had broken up with yesterday and who had called her this morning to see if she had come to her senses. "Do you want to meet?" she had asked Ana.

"No. I can't."

"Are you over there?"

"Headed there."

It had gone from bad to worse after that, but she was not the kind of person to lead anyone on.

"No. That's Jazz," she said out loud to no one as she entered the big kitchen with its pale yellow walls and big hand carved table. The two of them had taken such different relationship paths. Jasmine was not ready to settle down. She fucked but she didn't love. Sometimes Ana thought she was trying to see how many women she could bed in one weekend. It amazed her how gullible each one was, falling prey to those dark features and boyish bod one after the other. She, on-the-other-hand, had opted for two long term relationships, Marla over the last year and Danni. The first had lasted for several years while she was in college. It was easier when she had only seen Jasmine on breaks and without Danni in tow. Being back in Buxton and working in the art center in town made the lines blur. Ana and Jasmine saw each other regularly, in town, at the bar, alone for lunch.

As if on cue, Jasmine padded barefoot into the kitchen in all her unassuming beauty, wet strands of jet black hair across the lens of her glasses, the rest pulled back in a loose pony tail. She had her father's flannel shirt on, sleeves unbuttoned, tail hanging over a pair of black shorts. She looked at Ana and then around the room. "Where's Marla?"

"She isn't coming."

"What? She actually let you come alone into the lion's den?"

Ana didn't respond. Instead, she said, "Biscuits are getting cold," and nodded at the bag she had dropped onto the table. "Let's eat."

After they ate, they cleaned the house together, and went for a run on the beach. It felt good to Jasmine to be alone with Ana and to be out in the world again, if only for a few hours. Back at the house they took turns showering and heated leftovers from the fridge. Jasmine felt the darkness returning as they ate. It was the house. It swallowed her, consumed her, demanded that she remain in its belly.

After dinner, Ana moved to the soft leather sofa and patted the spot next to her. "Come on, Jazz."

Jasmine sat, pulled one leg up and tucked it under the other on the couch and turned to face her best friend.

"Jazz, the darkness is winning. I can't stand it."

"What does that even mean, Ana?" Jasmine was a dark soul by nature, Ana had known this about her from day one, and it kind of pissed her off that Ana was calling her out on it now.

"You know what I mean. This is different. I know you. Don't let his inability to cope ruin your chance for a life of your own Jasmine." It was a serious sort of whisper. She reached for Jasmine's empty hand. "It is time to let go of him, of her, of all of it. Sell the house. Go to Raleigh and complete your internship. Study the ocean floor. Dream. Love. Please, Jasmine. Please hear me."

Jasmine squeezed Ana's hand and looked into those soft denim-blue eyes that she loved so much. "I don't know if I can, or even if I fucking want to, Ana. Seriously. I will get through this. I always do. But going all the way to Raleigh? Selling the house? Leaving you and the beach and…?"

Ana cut her off. "You can. You have me. I will never leave you. It's a four-hour drive. Who knows, maybe I will live there someday, too."

"Bullshit. Marla will eventually get tired of our tug-of-war, and she will make you stay away. Then what? I only have you, Ana. Literally. And it fucking sucks." She wasn't sure why she was trying to hurt Ana's feelings, but she couldn't help it. It made her even madder that Ana didn't appear phased with her outburst.

Ana kept a steady low tone, never loosing eye contact. "He tied that rope Jasmine. He stood on the chair."

"They were together 19 years, Ana. 19. Fucking. Years."

"Yes, but his pain is not yours. You are strong and brave and alive."

"He chose her. Like you will choose Marla or someone else. Everyone that I love that deeply leaves me. It is what it fucking is. If I don't show the universe how I feel, it doesn't want to remove that person."

Ana's voice remained quiet, raspy. "Jasmine? I am still here. Is that why you have never crossed that line with me? Because you think I will leave, that the universe will take me? That's some serious fuckeduppidness, Jasmine. Damn it. I'm right here. I told Marla that I was in love with you, that I couldn't stay with her."

"What?"

"Six years I have waited for you to acknowledge us. Six. Fucking. Frustrating. Years."

"That was a stupid thing to tell her."

"That's all you have to say?" Ana looked back into eyes that were the exact opposite of her own light blue orbs: deep, brown, soulful.

Jasmine was devastated at the irresponsibility of a father that she loved, Ana knew that. She had stood by as Jasmine worked through the loss of her mom, and she was standing by her as she worked through the loss of her dad. Jasmine knew deep down that she would never leave her. In that moment, Jasmine knew something else, as well. This was her last chance to have this depth of love with another human being. Could she snub the universe and react before the moment was gone forever?

Ana felt her own voice crack. "Please?" Ana stared into her soul and held her hand.

Jasmine didn't look away. And neither did Ana.

"Ana?" Jasmine's heart beat faster. She leaned forward, put her hand to Ana's cheek. No turning back. Not tonight. Not ever again.

Jasmine kissed Ana gently at first, allowing the tingle of that first touch to linger in the tiny breath between them.

"Jasmine." Ana breathed her name against her lips. Jasmine answered by opening her mouth slightly, pushing harder against Ana's lips with her own, their tongues reaching, probing, until their breathing became labored and their sounds inaudible. Jasmine pulled back on the couch to look at Ana's face. The two already knew each other like they knew themselves. Jasmine's finger traced the curve of Ana's cheek, her neck. Their eyes were already fucking. Deep. Intense. Maddening. Jasmine's finger tracing the line of Ana's shoulder, arm, hand. "Come with me," she whispered.

As the sun began its journey into night and the fireflies began to dance across a watercolor sky, Jasmine and Ana stood face-to-face next to the bed. Lips seeking lips, ear lobes, chin, nibbling, biting. Jasmine eased her body back only enough to unbutton Ana's shirt. When it fell open she slid her hands inside, appreciating Ana's skin and her own in a brand new way. "I love you, Ana Grace. I have always loved you." She slid Ana's shirt off of her shoulders and to the ground. Ana gasped when she felt her bra strap open, her body responding to every move that the two of them made as Jasmine removed piece after piece of her clothing. As she slid Ana's jeans and panties toward the floor, Jasmine paused to kiss the flat of her stomach, her thigh, even her knee. She wanted to taste every tiny inch of Ana's tan slender frame. Returning to a standing position, Jasmine swallowed hard. A single tear ran down her cheek.

"Jasmine Esperanza. You are my best friend for life. And I will always be here to protect you." The words were barely audible, a gift from Ana to Jasmine.

"For life," Jasmine gave in return, picturing them together forever.

Over and over again through the night Ana and Jasmine fucked, licked, and sucked their way to ecstasy. Over and over again Jasmine fell in love with her best friend. Over and over again she let go of the fear of what could happen and just allowed herself to be right here, right now, with Ana.

As the sun came up, Ana looked again into Jasmine's eyes. "Let me tell you something, Jasmine Esperanza Castillo-Brookes. Your life has sometimes sucked, I mean sucked more than anyone's life I know. But *you* are not dead. *You* are still *alive*. Your mother lost her life to a stupid driver, and your dad lost his battle with grief, but you are alive and brave and worthy of life. So let's do each other a favor and remember that, ok?"

Jasmine thought back to the night the two of them had just shared. She could still smell Ana on her skin, still taste her on her lips. "I. Am. Alive." Jasmine said.

Ana cupped her hand to her ear and said, "Sorry, Can't hear you."

Jasmine stood up and positioned herself over Ana's lap as she sat on the edge of the bed, naked. Slowly, she bent forward, their faces inches apart. "I'm alive, Ana. With you, I'm alive."

Ana smiled. "That's better."

That night, Jasmine slept. It was the first time in years that she did not wake up, not once. It was a dreamless, quiet sleep. There were no demons, no shadows—only a hope for a future with the one woman that she loved enough to live for every day.

Raleigh, North Carolina, 2015

Ana stirred. Jasmine smiled. "How are you feeling? Do you need anything?"

"To see our daughter. And to kiss you. That's it."

"Happy to oblige, my lady." Jasmine stood, bent forward and down until their lips met, and whispered, "You are the most beautiful woman I have ever seen, and what you did today was amazing."

Ana looked at the love and light in Jasmine's eyes. Some days over the last eight years she had still seen moments of darkness, but not today. "She is beautiful, isn't she?"

As if on cue, Helen brought the sleeping baby to her mommas. "Do you two have a name for this tiny angel?" she asked as she handed the tightly wrapped infant to Jasmine.

Jasmine laid their daughter on Ana's breast. "What do think, my love? What should we name our daughter?"

"Esperanza Grace, I think," Ana whispered. "What do you think, little one?"

Jasmine touched her wife's cheek. She had never loved her more than she did in that instant, never loved anyone or anything more than she loved the two beings in front of her. She now understood her father's words. Loving Ana and little Esperanza was a calling, one she would never take for granted. "Esperanza Grace. My Spanish heritage smashing into your Anglo-Saxton roots." It's perfect.

Tammy Bird lives in Whitsett, North Carolina with her wife and two cats. She is an educator by day and a writer by night. Her passion for working with students and with words comes from her desire to describe life through storytelling and to show those around her the beauty of inclusivity. She has published several short stories and hopes to soon publish her first novel.

The Letter

Lucy J. Madison

Even though it was Friday night and still snowing outside after three days of a bone-chilling coastal storm, and even though he knew Sue would be waiting at home for him with a comforting pot roast dinner, Ray decided to clear out the back corner of the old Post Office. The edict that determined the Post Office would close its doors forever came down three months ago. Today had been the last day in nearly a century that the Falmouth Post Office on Cape Cod was open for business. He didn't want to get all sentimental but he would miss this place and he still took pride in making sure even this final job of cleaning the place out was done, and done well.

Ray continued to stack the old and useless metering equipment on a dolly so he could haul it into the dumpster outside. After about ten minutes, he worked up a good sweat and stopped for a moment to catch his breath. As he took off his heavy flannel shirt, he looked around at the place where he spent the last twenty years. He loved this place like a person. It had character, this old post office, but like a lot of things these days, it had been deemed useless. The old post office closed permanently only to be replaced by some sterile and cold state-of-the-art modern facility in the next town over.

Something on the floor caught his eye. Dropping

the damp shirt on the dolly, and Ray bent down to see what it was. Underneath years of dirt and dust, Ray found a letter. Marred with dozens of brown splotches from the leaky radiator, the dry yellowed envelope almost crinkled in his hand. It was not unusual to lose a letter here and there, but this one felt different. This one looked different. For starters, the address did not have a zip code on it, which was a clear indication that the letter was at least fifty years old. The name and address were written in sharp, looping letters slanted downward.

He strained to read the name on the envelope but after a few minutes under a florescent proofing light, made out the name Julia McDaniels. His eyes scanned the letter for any clues. Finally, he made out the postmark in the faded red ink that read: Boston, Massachusetts 1944.

"World War II," he said aloud, "Jesus, it's a war letter!" Ray turned the letter over and over in his hands as if he had found a fragile glass Christmas ornament. He wanted desperately to open the letter and read its contents, but he didn't dare. This was not his letter to open. This was not his story to tell. He was merely the messenger, and he had an urgent special delivery to make.

He knew the recipient. Hell, everyone in Falmouth knew Julia McDaniels. She was as much a part of Falmouth and Cape Cod as sand on the beach. She was a tough old bird in her early 90s who rarely asked for help and rarely needed it. An English teacher for over 40 years, Ms. McDaniels taught Ray and just about every other local for two generations everything from Shakespeare and D.H. Lawrence to proper comma placement and subject/noun agreement. Ray carefully packed the letter in a clear plastic bag, grabbed his coat and car keys, and headed for the door.

❧❧❧❧

Julia eyed the faded yellow letter all afternoon, thinking it would, and probably should, miraculously disappear once again to the mysterious corner of the old post office from which it had come. Ray was the grandson of the butcher Julia knew as a child. He was the sweet boy who loved A.A. Milne and J.R.R. Tolkien. Ray delivered the letter yesterday like it was a fragile, precious stone. Julia always remembered her students by the books and authors they loved to read as children. She could tell by the way Ray reverently handed her the letter that he thought it was something magical, some special gift from the cosmos that might save her or set her free. She only smiled and nodded her thanks to him, not wanting her eyes to betray the fact that she knew better. She knew the letter and its contents would only remind her of what once was and what should have been. This was not a welcome gift at all.

As she stared unwavering and unblinking at the letter, the thought occurred to her that she should burn it unread; send it away with all the other memories that were unfinished and hidden, locked somewhere deep inside and untouched for so long. But for all her internal bluster, she did not burn it. She did not open it. She just stared at it and puzzled over its timing and its contents. She had waited fifty-one years for this letter. It had been so long, she almost forgot what she had been waiting for. Almost.

Julia carried the letter with her into the bathroom. She inhaled sharply as her feet touched the ice cold tile. She ran a scalding hot bath, adding epsom salt and lavender to the water. As she bathed, she closed her eyes and dreamed someone else's hands were upon her. It was a familiar dream. Each night as her body aged and withered, she dreamed her hands were not her own as the water rinsed the day away. That much had not changed in fifty-one years, and she doubted it would change if she read the contents of that letter.

After her bath, she retired to bed, carefully placing the letter on the pillow beside her. She turned onto her side and tucked her hand beneath her head. All night long she stared at the letter as the wind howled outside. All night long she remembered a different time when life was simple and filled with the sweet scent of possibility and hope. Possibility and hope are wasted on the young, she thought. So is sleep, apparently.

In the murky pre-dawn light, Julia rose slowly from her bed. Getting up was the most difficult part of any day and today was no different. The old floorboards groaned and creaked just like her bones as she slowly moved from one end of the room to the other.

Julia pulled the dark brown wool sweater over her head and she looked in oval full length mirror that was once her mother's. Usually she ignored herself, but today she felt different. Her dark green eyes lifted to the old woman reflected across from her. In that split second before her eyes met her own, she half-expected to see someone young, strong, and vibrant, look back at her with haughty confidence and a quick wit. Instead, the old and weathered face she saw was lined and worn like a true New Englander. This woman looked at her, through her, with a beaten smile and a tilted chin. She stared at herself and saw how hard and cold she looked. She thought she looked almost dead inside. In that moment she realized that she hadn't won in her battle against time. Time beat her. She couldn't bear to look any longer at her own face so she twisted her coarse gray hair back in a bun and finished dressing as quickly as possible.

Toast and tea would calm her, she thought. Although she knew she would not touch either. She just stared out the window at the sea as the toast and tea cooled in front of her. She heard the familiar sound of the grandfather clock in the living room that her grandfather built with his own two hands. Tick. Tock. Julia closed her eyes and with each tick, feel the warmth of the sun. With each tock, stood at the doorway and watched as she made love to someone from so long ago. Whenever she closed her eyes, another memory was back at the edges of her memory, taunting her. Every time she opened her eyes, the emptiness and silence surrounded her like a blanket.

She carefully tucked the letter into her parka's pocket as she bundled up for a walk. A walk on the beach would clear her head, she thought. Even though it was February and a brutal Nor'Easter had been blowing for days, Julia knew she needed the beach to calm her. It was where she made every major decision of her life and deciding what to do with this letter required that same attention. She walked down the wooden boardwalk from the house that had been in her family for three generations. She continued onto the beach to an old Adirondack chair just above the high tide line and sat down. The wind died down and the sky was streaked with hues of blues and pinks and yellows. Even the waves were calm and gentle once again, although the cold chilled her to the bone.

As Julia stared out at the winter sea, she felt surprised again at the speed of time. Her daughter,

Annie, left for Boston University when she was eighteen, and moved on to her life in the city, never to return to Falmouth. While they speak every day, and see each other often, Annie's inevitable leaving created a void that Julia never really grew accustomed to.

Julia adopted and raised Annie by herself, and it was always just the two of them, here at the beach. Annie was her blond angel. Everyone in the small Cape Cod coastal town liked them well enough, Annie was impossible not to like. She was smart, beautiful and wonderfully funny. But there was always the suspicion. A mother and daughter without a husband always raised suspicion, particularly back then. Over time, the folks in town grew used to Julia and Annie, and let them alone. Julia spent the best years of her life teaching English, writing, and raising Annie. Her life was full of her students, her books, and her daughter. But each night she retired to an empty bedroom and each morning, she woke to the empty side of the bed as a constant reminder, as a penance. She would pay for the decisions she made and was afraid to make.

The wind chilled her even through the wool sweater and down parka. Her legs ached and her ears were going numb. She made her decision. She would read the letter. She tore open the envelope and read:

April 12, 1944

Dear Jules:

It has been a year. I have tried to forget you ever existed, but I cannot. There is this war raging in my heart and in the world. I still try to understand why you just walked away without even saying goodbye but I cannot.

I believe that people come into our lives to teach us lessons, and to help us understand the miracle in simply being alive. I am so thankful that you were ever in my life at all, even though I wish that sometimes I could forget you and go back to the time before I met you. I know now that you are the greatest lesson of my life. By loving you, I will learn patience. I will learn heartache. I am learning that the greatest love is expecting absolutely nothing in return.

You are my first thought upon waking, my last thought before sleeping. Everything I see or hear or feel reminds me somehow of you. I want to be the one to make you smile, to make you laugh, to be there without judgment when things are difficult, and to be there to celebrate all of the accomplishments I know you will experience in your lifetime. I want to cook for you, care for you, and nurture all that you are, but if you do not want me to be that person for you, then I hope you find someone who can give you those gifts. I want to kiss you and tell you that you are loved and desired, and I want you to be strengthened by my love. Yet if you do not want me to be that person for you, I hope with all my heart you find someone who can give you those gifts. I want to make love to you and show you a passion so unrelenting, so deep that it shakes you to your core and brings you to heights you never thought existed, but if you do not want me to be the one to give you that pleasure, I hope with all my heart you find someone who does.

I will wait as long as it takes for you to come back to me. I will stuff aside the ache of wanting to find you, to touch you once again. I will hammer down the hatches of my heart for the rest of my life if that is what you ask of me. I am yours, and you have my heart to do with it what you will. In that way, we are tethered together forever, even if we never speak another word to one another.

I still dream of you sweetheart and I suspect for

the rest of my life. In my dreams, it is always summer, your favorite season. You lie on your stomach in the sun and I watch you turn the color of spun gold as the waves crash against the shore.

I know you are afraid of what we have. So am I, but I know this: I want to spend the rest of my life with you, damn the consequences. I don't care what other people think. I don't care that they will stare and wonder why we aren't married to men. We have each other and that is enough. It was always enough for me.

I love you Jules. I always will. You may will yourself to forget me. You may live a life without me in it. It's been a year and I wonder if you found someone else to love you, but I know that no one will ever love you the way I do. Maybe you found someone you can walk down a street with and not be ashamed of. I think one day you will have a daughter and her name will be Annie. I remember you telling me once how you loved that name. She will be the colors of the sun and sky, golden hair with blue eyes.

I have thought many times that I should just return to the beach and find you, because I know you will be there, but I also know this is your choice. If you read this letter and still feel that we cannot be together, I will respect that wish. I will never agree with it, but I will respect it. But if you read this letter and your heart opens again, find me sweetheart, because I will be waiting for you.

I am yours forever and always.
Rebecca

After she read the letter for the third time, Julia stood up and walked to the water. Without ceremony, she dropped the letter and the envelope into the water.

She let the sea take it all away. She could not even cry. All this time later, and she could not even cry.

All these years gone by and Julia assumed Rebecca never wrote to her because of her damned pride. Impulsive, beautiful Rebecca. The long, slender hands she dreamt of. The impossibly long eyelashes, the quick wit, those dark chocolate eyes. She never forgot any of it. Yet, as the years flew by, she grew bitter and angry, believing it was Rebecca's pride that kept them apart, not her own mistake in leaving. Julia willfully chose a life alone, never to love again, never to make love again, as penance for hurting her beloved Rebecca. Julia realized it was her own stubbornness that had won. Her fear of being judged had become her sole remaining lover.

This letter came now, after the war in her heart was long over. She knew now she lost the battle, made the wrong decision that warm day in April when she left Rebecca sleeping. They were lovers for long enough to know there would never be anyone else who would ever touch her heart and soul the way Rebecca had. Yet even in knowing that, she chose to sneak silently out of the room like a coward, believing she was saving them both a life of heartache and trouble. People would never understand a love like theirs. They would never be able to live openly and share their love with the world. Looking back one last time to see Rebecca's dark curly hair cascading down the pillow and off the bed, Julia made the decision without ever telling Rebecca, and that single stupid decision changed the trajectory of both their lives forever. Julia believed that since they had to hide their love, it was somehow not worth keeping or fighting for. She was wrong. How could she have been so wrong?

Now at 91 years old, Julia realized for the first time

that the bulk of her life was predicated on a mistake–
her mistake. The substance of her entire life hinged
on an error in her own judgment, a flaw inside herself
that kept her, and Rebecca, from living a life of love,
laughter, and happiness together. That knowledge,
that final understanding, was almost more than Julia
could bear. She literally felt the last remaining piece
of her heartbreak for the final time inside her chest. If
she had only received this letter when it was sent. If it
hadn't been lost. If she hadn't been so stupid. All these
ifs amounted to a pile of nothing like sand through her
fingertips.

She watched Rebecca's words disappear as the
paper rocked to and fro until it sank beneath the surface
of the ice-cold water. A whole life lost, Julia thought,
almost surprised, as she walked back toward the house,
hugging herself against the cold February chill.

*Lucy J. Madison is an author, screenwriter, and poet. Her
work often delves into the intricacies of relationships,
passion, and love. She resides with her wife of 16 years in
Connecticut and in Provincetown, MA along with their
beloved pets.*

Website: www.lucyjmadison.com

The One

Stephanie Kusiak

When I was eight-years-old, I dreamed of her. I know exactly how that sounds…I'm a realist. I look at the world like a dog-eat-dog kind of place where the only good you ever get is the good you make by beating the crap out of everyone else. Not physically, mind you, but certainly in prowess, skills and smarts. I'm a killer in a board room, the go-to when something needs getting done.

However, that doesn't negate the fact that when I was eight-years-old, I had a dream of a woman with dark tumbling hair and a height just enough to make me tip my head up when she kissed me. Someone whose arms could come around me and mute the bad, sad, miserable feelings I felt. And I did feel them, terrible painful things, that didn't make any sense in a dream where I was kissing someone who seemed to mean so much to me.

I didn't understand those feelings, not back then. Not when I was a little kid whose existence was wrapped up in what adventure my 'My Little Ponies' would have that day. Gratefully, I lived a life where the bad things were shielded until I was old enough to learn, old enough to feel pain, and live with it in spades. Until it made me hard, and bitter, and hurt in ways I can't even fully describe without wincing.

No, back in those days I just awoke with phantoms

of feelings I didn't understand, and a twisted expression of confusion as to why I was kissing a girl. Years passed, and I figured out the latter part, figured out why I was kissing a girl in that dream. The only thing that eluded me was the long standing question of *who* I had been kissing for so many years.

And whether it was conscious or not, I looked for her. I dated people, kissed them, closed my eyes and felt for the 'fit' from my dream. I stared into their eyes and asked silently if they were the person I'd been waiting for. I'd never seen her face, so my blind hunt lingered on feeling alone. And I gave it my all, as I'm wont to do, throwing everything I had to give into one grinder and then the next, wishing and waiting for the next brunette to be *her*. It was when I was finally battered and bruised, when the very idea of compromising the sanctity of my heart was enough deterrent to keep me from doing it, that I gave up completely.

I consciously settled for someone far less than what I wanted.

Because that girl–woman–wasn't real.

And I am a realist who accepts that a happy ending can only exist in the mind and heart of a little eight-year-old girl.

Besides, I had better things to do that vivisect my heart over and over like an idiot.

More years passed, divorce happened, because it's hard to play love with the wrong person willfully. Faux affection is hollow comfort on the cold edge of the bed. It's a cold that is somehow far more than cold when juxtaposed against that same dream, over and over, a twisted ode to the unobtainable.

Someone I would never have.

Yet, something I would spend my whole life

looking for.

Masochism knows no bounds like a woman in love with an ideal.

I believed that for a very long time, believed in my heart of hearts that there couldn't be anything more painful than wishing for someone I'd never find. I figured that I was doomed to walk through life one vacant step at a time. I'd find my peace in small moments, the in-between instances where happiness came up and bubbled from some place within me.

I was so wrong.

I was wrong about where happiness would find me, since it now fills me from the inside out and ripples smiles to my face that squeeze my cheeks to the aching. The steps I take patterned beside equal steps, warm and familiar with solidity and reality.

I was wrong to believe she didn't exist.

And I was wrong to believe there couldn't be anything more painful than never finding her.

I can testify to something worse as I lay in the dark, in our bedroom where it holds me tight enough to make the tears hurt less. The only thing that hurts worse than not finding the person you were meant to love, is finding them and having to leave them over and over again. It's the pain of knowing every time I fly to see her, there's a silent timer on our visit, a tick down toward the inevitable parting. That I smile, and I laugh, but I know there is a finite measure on those smiles and laughs until we meet again.

I know–I should be grateful I found her at all. I know I should count myself lucky to be lying right here in her arms, with that softness of her shoulder catching my tears. I know all of that.

I *know*.

But I'm not the kind of woman that is satisfied with 'half way' or 'almost there,' just like I'm not satisfied with the at-least-you-found-her placation.

So, I lay here in the dark and feel her warmth. I feel how right it is to breathe her in and I cry because when morning comes I'll have to catch my flight and leave. I stare at her profile; memorize it against the dusty threat of daylight. It's a ritual, an obsession, and a pleasure all in one. She hates her nose, so that's what I pay the most attention to. I love it more in make up for her loathing. If I didn't think I'd wake her, I'd kiss it over and over.

And though I don't think she'd particularly mind being woken by kisses, she has to work in the morning, and I love her enough to let her sleep despite the agony I feel in silence.

Because, she's my one.

I've told it to her at least a handful of times, sometimes with booming laughter and in other times with quiet reverence, but I mean it…more than I've meant anything in my whole life. What she doesn't know, is that when I say it, it carries the weight of thirty years of dreaming of her. It comes with the weight of grinding my heart into pieces on the millstone of others' disregard. It's a declaration in promise to my heart as much as it's a mantle for her to wear.

She is my one.

I cling to that, press my wet temple and face to the warmth of her sleeping shoulder and hopelessly try to cover the cold of my future emptiness with the solid, real heat of her. But it's always in vain, always futile, as the march of time draws cruel nails in the soft, fleshy parts of my heart.

And because it cannot be stopped, it's not long before I'm kissing her goodbye on the sidewalk.

I kiss her like her lips will be the first thing I forget when we are apart. They're soft, unassuming lips, far too unassuming for the intimacy in which they know me. They are kind in their inspection, perhaps because she knows that one more ounce of pressure, one more millimeter of depth, and her kiss will break the flimsy resolve that keeps me returning to my job and my life far away from her.

And in this goodbye kiss I ask myself again, why am I leaving? Why can't I just quit my job and live on my savings till I find something else? Why can't I just leave my condo and live with her? Why can't I just cut every tie that holds me bound to a place out of her embrace?

My answer is in the look of her eyes when our lips part. It's in that deep brown that sparkles with tears and love alike in the glow of the terminal lights and a terminal dawn. It's in the fact that I know her love is partly founded on my seeming maturity, because I'm steadfast and brave, and oh so different from the others before me. Those rash fools that ran with bladed words and impaled them into her heart. She loves me with the completeness of an unfiltered existence, and it's in the Catch 22 security I exemplify that I get to have her in the first place. I have no choice but to leave, to have her.

And when her eyes spill, I tug her closer. My fingers ungainly caress and twine her cream scarf. I make a pattern of the fringe to alleviate the disorder I cannot resolve in my heart.

"I love you." That nose I love so much touches mine, brushing tears to my skin.

"I love you, too." My voice holds firm. I already cried out all my tears last night. "I'll see you soon, in like, a month."

She only nods, her lip trembling. We've said the

word 'soon' as many times as one might be able to stomach in a lifetime. It doesn't provide the comfort it used to after six months of fruitless job searches and attempted promotions. The word soon is a brass ring seemingly out of reach.

I press another kiss to her lips, this time it's salted with sorrow. "Don't cry. I'm not actually leaving. I'm right here, I'm right here with you always."

Her hands firm, like they're feeling and remembering me. They grasp to hold the tactile whisper I'm about to become. "I know."

But we both know it isn't true.

I am leaving. I'm about to board a plane and fly out of her city, out of her proximity. I'm about to be too far away to share a kiss, a hug. I won't be able to glance at her and flash a smile. In thirty minutes, I'll be lined up to be gone–despite my heart screaming for me not to be. She must think the same, reach the same realization, when a look passes over her face that mirrors the ache I feel in my chest.

But then it's gone, like the wind blew the emotive dust off her polished propriety. She's braver than I will ever be. I tease that it's her 'ninja training' where she can deftly manipulate the substance of her emotions until even her tears dry like they never existed at all. Where she can even put a genuine smile on her face and nudge me a little with a laugh.

"Go on. Get out of here before I make you stay."

She moves away, all long lines and the beautiful cut of a black pea coat. And my God, she doesn't know how desperately I want her to tell me to stay. I'd give my anything, *anything*, for it. I beg her silently to say it.

God, please just say it.

Please say you *want* to keep me as badly as I want

to stay.

I put my hand on my suitcase's handle and the click of it tipping onto its wheels seems to stop her. She turns back to me at the end of her car. Those dark eyes meet mine, stare me down as the lights paint a stark bas relief of dark hair, black coat, and the porcelain of her skin. I tug the heavy case toward me, fighting the threat of more tears.

"I dare you to make me stay." I whisper, moving slowly away. She smiles, so I press again even as I keep moving. "I dare you to *let* me stay." This time I say it breathlessly enough that she pushes another smile that turns into a hiss of pain and the crumble of her expression.

In seeing that, I know she would if she could. However, I have no right to ask this of her. I have no right to beg and plead and implore her to tell me to stay. The same way I can't ask her to move down near me, leave her job, abandon the authentic life she's creating far away from the barbed tradition of her Asian family…I can't ask her to make the demands of me I cannot make in return. We're stuck at an impasse, where the slow warble of her breath will come through a phone's speaker and soothe me to sleep.

And in knowing that, until that elusive 'soon' comes I need to make these goodbyes gentler on her heart.

So, I smile.

I smile with a tilt fof my head and a crooked grin that not even a day ago, had her pressing kisses to my cheeks until I giggled. "It's cold, silly girl. Get in the car. Want me to call when I get back?"

She scoffs, fingers wiping beneath her eyes. "Is that even a question?"

"No." I soothe. "I love you."

"I love you, too."

I rush inside, holding the tatters of my resolve. Despite the dedication in my steps, my traitorous heart has me turning to look back at her, catching a flash of her desperate breath from the inside of the car. Then, the automatic doors seal before me, closing me off from her and the home I've grown to love.

I don't know why it is that suddenly I've arrived at a point of no return, where walking back through the door isn't an option. I wonder about that as empty steps carry me to the escalator. I ride it up to the security checkpoint, blind to the people around me; they make typical lines in a multitude of colors and shapes. I assume my place, walking the long, naked row reserved for frequent fliers. A title I've earned purely on the merits of our combined financial prowess and my resolve to steal every moment I can to be with her.

I tighten my hand on the strap of the bag over my shoulder and lower my chin. I brace for the walk, brace against the image of last night, of her swirling chestnut hair and warmth pressed into my side. I steady myself for the memory of her sleeping breath brushing my wet cheek and the lingering scent of her perfume tickling my nose. Her arm holding me tightly even in sleep.

I remember the day before that, where her laughs punctuated the image of her over me and the flutter of sheets swathed us like some kind of dream. I remember those kisses on my crooked grin, and how they eventually melted into the gentlest movement of her lips as she laid in my arms.

Never in all my life has something that felt so right, left me with feelings of such wrong. And though I've passed the point of no return, though the eyes of the security agents are measuring my movements, I stop.

I stop and I remember my dream.

I let it all wash through me right there in the A list lane. Her touch, her hair between my fingers, the way I tilt my head just a slight bit to catch warm, soft lips. I let it all wash through me that I've waited *thirty years* for her. That those abstract feelings I didn't understand as a child are the threads of regret and loss that stitch my throat closed with a lump today. That I'm an idiot to think that one more day, *one more hour*, is a fair down payment on a future breath I cannot guarantee.

All I can guarantee is now and there is no amount of money or security worth the time I'm wasting it on.

And God damn it, thirty years is *enough*.

I turn sharply, a surprised gasp on the lips of the person I brush past. I push my way to the platform area where passengers corral themselves into security lanes. My hands tighten on my luggage and I force my way through. Hasty apologies litter from my lips, disingenuous and fleeting. I don't know why it took so many trips, so much heartbreak to realize…I have somewhere else to be.

It's the place in her arms that has tangled my life with hers and strangled the tears from my heart every flight home.

Down the escalator, my bag slamming out the steps. Plastic on metal banging for the world to hear, for them all to know, this is my choice. They echo in testament to the fact I don't have to be a hopeless romantic to pick love above everything else, I can be a realist, with my skills as a commodity to be traded to the highest bidder.

That is a trade I'm willing to make, an opportunity cost not too high in it's paying. But her? Her in that car with a shaken breath and tears in her eyes?

It's too much to pay for both her and I.

Because…this is where I belong.

The cold morning hits like a hammer, I cough, sputter as I hunt between the streaming bodies heading toward the ticketing counters and baggage check. Her car is gone, not sitting idle where she left me. Damn it.

Why didn't I just stay?

I drop the bag on my shoulder, the weight too heavy to carry under the realization that I'm too late. I stare at it, at its near empty pack job because I leave everything of mine here, every time. With a twinge of pain I clear my throat and stare down the street realizing I might as well leave despite my blustery realizations.

Then, I see her, held at a red light. It hits me square in the chest, because she must have waited so long for me to turn around and come back. Or sat and cried knowing I wouldn't. My hand tightens on the phone in my pocket. It's now or never, despite other chances to do this same dance—what I do right now will echo wide and lasting between us. The fact I've come this far is enough of a realization for me.

There are no 'take-backs' on this desperate attempt to stay and the words I can feel building up in my throat.

The light turns green as I dial her number and hit send.

Say it or don't?

It rings.

Go back to my job, or find another one here with her?

The line connects and the first words out of my mouth are the thing I commit to.

"Don't leave."

I watch the dark gray SUV jerk to the right without

question.

And as I rush toward her, everything I've been trying to say ripping from me in plumes of breath.

"I know we've talked about being responsible. I know this is crazy. I know you want steady and stable. I know you want me to be brave enough to do this. But I can't keep leaving you. I can't do it." I stop outside the car, her red-rimmed eyes holding mine through the glass. And for a split second I can hear myself in stereo as she leans across to open the door. "I have loved you for longer than I've known you. And, God, I know I shouldn't sacrifice our future for the present, but I just can't go. I'm supposed to be here with you."

She opens her mouth and nothing comes out. But then it does, when the tears fill her eyes.

"You're insane, and I love you. Get in the car right this moment, so I can kiss you and take you home."

Growing up in Orange County, CA, Stephanie Kusiak spent her formative years climbing trees with her brothers, rescuing stray animals and learning all she could about the supernatural from her grandmother over the traditional 'Pancake Sunday.' As a writer, she strives to capture the humanizing elements that dot life and focuses on building vibrant characters. When not writing, Stephanie enjoys her work as a Corporate Training Analyst within the financial industry and flying to the Bay Area to spend time her fiancée.

Old Habits, New Beginnings

N.R. Dunham

I need to go. I need to go!"

I look up from my place between Jess's legs, feel myself smirking in that way she loves or loathes depending on the day. "I know I'm rather good at this, but I've never heard your words go backwards like that. Nice compliment." Scratching lightly along the inside of Jess's thigh, I go back to what I was doing.

She swears at me, lets out a moan, and then pulls on my hair. Normally I'm fine with this. I've been fine for the last twenty minutes at least, but Jess usually has the awareness to check her grip. Woman can't tell if she needs to come or go, and now she's scalping me. This time I'm the one swearing at her.

"Well. For fuck's sake, Skyler, you're not listening!"

Jess is flushed from her cheek down to her neck. This can mean arousal or anger. I'm guessing both right now, but why she's pissed I have no idea. "Listening to what?" I ask, soothing the place where a few more hair strands used to reside.

"I need to go."

"You do not. It's early, and we—"

"I need to go to Reno."

I pause, finally look at her properly. She's beautiful, long hair flowing past her shoulders and stopping just above her nipples, which are appealingly hard. I want to congratulate myself for that, and for the extra color in her face, but she's staring at me oddly enough that patting myself on the back doesn't seem the right move. "Okay," I reply, drawing out the word. I'm trying to buy time, figure out this glaringly obvious thing that I'm not getting. "So, we have to talk about this now? When are you going, next week, next month?"

It's not that I don't care. I do, and I'll miss Jess like crazy. But absence makes the heart grow fonder and the reunion fucking is fucking amazing. Jess leaves more often than she doesn't, spends more time in hotels than she does her apartment. It's her thing, she goes from one underperforming hotel to the next, whips the place into shape, then comes back with her tacky presents from resort gift shops and her fabulous reunion sex. It's the way of things, of us. I wish she'd gotten to stick around longer this time, more than I'll ever admit (that would be against our arrangement), but I'll live with it. I still don't understand why this couldn't wait, not when she's naked except for that half-open silk blouse.

"Jesus. Skyler. Eyes up here."

She snaps her fingers at me. And she's used my proper name twice. I roll my wandering eyes and study her face again. "You're not the Dog Whisperer, Jessica, so quit with the finger thing. And if you hadn't interrupted the finger thing I've been practicing just for you, I wouldn't—"

"Skye. I'm not…I wouldn't be coming back."

Oh. Well. She's got my attention now. After pressing me about the eye contact, her gaze is suddenly downward, away from me. Still I feel vulnerable, exposed. I cover my breasts, change my mind, and drop the hand that'd been toying with Jess's clit to the duvet, wiping it clean. My sheets are a tangled mess. I root through them, finding the pants I'd thrown aside earlier. This is the kind of conversation that requires pants.

She talks while I dress. Her boss wants to put her somewhere more permanent with a better salary. She tells me about this latest hotel that needs saving. I catch maybe half of her words. She re-buttons that lovely blouse as she speaks, moves to hide herself under the covers. I hand her the shorts I tore off her when I came in. I kind of want to throw them at her, but that would be childish and bitchy.

"Good timing," I say, fiddling with the bedspread as I sit in front of her. More clothing didn't help with the vulnerability.

Jess's shrug is both helpless and apologetic, two traits I don't generally associate with her. "You were in a really good mood. Didn't want to wreck it. But I couldn't stop thinking about it, couldn't relax enough for—"

"Yeah, I got it."

"Sorry."

"Don't be. No reason for it."

It's true. I basically attacked Jess the minute I saw her. The game development firm I work for just approved my latest pitch, the one I've been honing and nerding out over for years. I got so excited that I couldn't see how Jess wasn't. I'm an ass. Especially because I'm a little relieved that it was her stress causing the problem. Losing my best friend and my touch in the same day would be too depressing, winning pitch or not.

"Dammit. Sorry I jumped you."

Jess tries to laugh. "Never been something you had to be sorry for."

"No. But it looks like things are changing."

I'm pathetic. I sound pathetic because I am pathetic. Jess takes my hand, speaks quietly. "I don't know what to do."

That catches me off-guard, almost as much as Reno did. I squeeze her hand, search blue eyes. "I think you made it obvious that you need to go."

"Come on, Skye."

"What?"

"I want the job. It's a great opportunity. Everything I've worked for since college."

"So?"

"So, that doesn't mean I want to leave…this."

"This" I presume, is me, us, maybe but Jess won't say that. Against the arrangement. The one that says we keep things casual, open. The one that's supposed to keep us from having conversations like this. I don't want her to leave this either. But I'd know how badly she wanted this job even if she hadn't just told me. I think of my videogame, the one that seems very trivial right now. The character sketches, the coding, all the work. What if I had to walk away from that? It would hurt like hell, and I'm not even half the workaholic Jess is.

"Hey," I tell her, leaning in to cup her cheek with my free hand. "You do whatever you need to do. I'm always here, you know that, and I will not be the reason you miss out on being some fabulously successful badass. More than you already are, I mean."

"I'd never want to hurt you."

I kiss her, quicker then I normally would. Pull her in close, rub her back. "Nothing that's good for you would hurt me. Promise."

I hold the embrace; drop a few kisses to her shoulder, the side of her neck. Jess hugs me back, shows no signs of pulling away any time soon. That's good. She can't see me from this angle, can't read my face. If she could, she'd know that I'm lying.

※ ※ ※ ※

I watch Jess pack up the last of her stuff, things left at my apartment God knows how long ago. A hairbrush, some DVD's, books she loaned that I'd finished long ago and never bothered to properly return. Jess gives me a tight smile as she packs the suitcase laid out on my bed,

Our living arrangements have been a tangled mess for as long as I've known her. Two separate spaces that might as well have been one, considering how long I spent in her home and her in mine. We met in college, courtesy of Emma, Jess's slutty roommate. Emma had a different guy in their room every week, which meant she wanted Jess out of it. The Jess of today wouldn't stand for that, but six or seven years ago, different story. She let herself be exiled and I came across her during a late night at the library. I'm an insomniac. My roommate had a strict lights out time and freaked with every one of my tosses and turns. If the dorm assignments were different, if Jess and I were brave enough then to reclaim our sides of the rooms, I wonder what I'd be doing right now, who I'd be with. As thought exercises go, it's not pleasant.

"You sure I can't drop you at the airport?" I know what she'll say, I'm just talking to fill the silence, distract myself from the reality of her leaving tomorrow.

She smiles wider as she zips up her suitcase. It doesn't reach her eyes. "You have work."

I shrug. "I'll get sick."

"That'll look great. Play hooky just when your pet project, your *dream* project, gets off the ground. Good strategy."

"You think I can't catch up on a few hours? Thanks for the massive underestimating."

She pauses, locks eyes with me. Her gaze is like a physical thing. "I've never underestimated you. Never have, never will."

I want to kiss her. Or shake her. Tell her she can't say things like that while looking at me like that, not anymore. In college, we bonded over crappy roommates and commitment issues, sharing amusing but horrifying anecdotes about our respectively broken homes. She made fun of my name. I don't remember exactly when we started having sex, only that Emma was quite pissed when we kicked her out of Jess's room that first time. Not the typical definition of revenge sex, but it was glorious nonetheless.

I wish it'd just been about sex sometimes. That would've been easier. There were always feelings involved, the typical friends with benefits thing was never going to work. Didn't seem like anything else would either. We tried once or twice, but the timing was always off. School or work or some other crush, always something. And when Jess started changing locales every few months, then came the arrangement. The one where we stopped trying to force things, saw each other when we could, dated others when we couldn't.

It suddenly occurs to me that despite the option being there, I haven't seen anyone else in a long time, even when Jess was gone for nearly a year at her last placement. The realization stalls my breathing. Jess starts talking, heaving her luggage off my bed as she does.

"Anyway, airports are evil, and I can't have you chasing after me like in those damn rom coms. Begging me not to leave, declaring undying devotion and all that."

She passes me as she wheels her things out of my

bedroom. I follow, rolling my eyes and hoping she can't tell that she's on to something. "Right. I was just going to buy you a latte then dump you on the curb. Since you're being such an arrogant smartass though, no latte."

"Do not chase me through the airport," she says as if I hadn't spoken. "Just don't. If the TSA people take it the wrong way and you go to airline prison just because you couldn't let go of me—"

"Airline prison?" I repeat, letting the banter play out. Jess sucks at goodbyes. I suck at goodbyes. It's probably better this way. "What are you even talking about?" Her jacket is draped over my couch. I help her slip into it as she stops in front of my door.

"I don't know. Think I'm still recovering from the pre-packing stuff."

I chuckle. Against every rule she has about business before pleasure, we'd fucked before packing. Sex with Jess was always good, but this was spectacular. And terribly depressing. "You sure you'll be okay to get yourself on the plane? No chaperone required?"

"It'll be tough, but I'll manage."

"Text me when you land."

"Always do."

I nod, searching for something to say. I'm still struggling when Jess lets go of her suitcase, pulling me in for the tightest of hugs.

"I'm so proud of you," she says in my ear, then pulls back a bit, stroking my cheek. "Your game. I think I forgot to tell you that."

"You didn't forget, but thanks. And right back at you." It's not a lie. I'm beyond proud of her. I focus on that, not the stupid, selfish part of myself that's hurt and pissed that she's leaving.

Jess is the one who nods this time. Then she kisses

me. It's slow, and lasts so long that I start to lose my breath. Still, I have to bite back a sound of protest when she breaks the contact. She speaks into my ear again. "Bye, baby."

I shiver. We don't do pet names much, not outside the bedroom. The unexpected words, her breath so close, they render me speechless and immobile. By the time I even think to do something about that, Jess is already gone.

❦ ❦ ❦ ❦

She texts me when she lands. After that, barely anything. Two one sentence e-mails, a picture of her new living room, and one-ten second voicemail. It's not abnormal. When she's settling into a new place, Jess is usually hard to get in touch with. I should be too busy to notice. The game's taking nearly all of my time. I rarely answer my calls anyway, so I shouldn't notice her radio silence.

I notice.

I almost contact her a handful of times, but don't. She's probably buried under the weight of her job, I'm definitely buried in mine, and I need to get used to this permanent absence.

More than a month after Jess leaves, I'm hunched over my laptop, ignoring the pull of my bed. Just because I'm sitting on it doesn't mean I can afford to sleep. It's past three in the morning and I might be going a little blind. I'm tired, but my mind doesn't care and trying to sleep just leads to a marathon session of staring at the ceiling. If I'm going to be up all night I can at least be productive about it.

Except I'm not. Somehow I've clicked away from

my work program and found Jess's Facebook page. This would be ridiculous even if it didn't make me look like a pining twelve-year-old. Jess isn't one to over share online and either way, I can't be one of those crazy people who stalk their ex's Facebook. Except I am. I'm disgusting myself. I scan her page. Whole lot of nothing, which is what I deserve for stooping this low. Jess's last bit of activity was to inform anyone reading that she was living in Reno now. I'm trying not to scowl at the screen when my phone rings. I get rid of the page, as if Jess can see that I've been snooping. And it *is* Jess; I'd know that without the custom ringtone. No one else would call this late. Thrilled and terrified, I reach over to my nightstand, grabbing my cell.

"Why aren't you sleeping?"

Jess talks before I can. "You woke me up."

"Liar. You're never this coherent after I wake you up. And you were on Facebook two seconds ago."

Fuck. Shutting the laptop I set it aside, leaning back against the pillows. "Shouldn't you be running the next Trump Tower or something? What are you doing on Facebook?"

"Multitasking. And don't bring Trump's name into this, it's insulting."

"Ah. Please do forgive me for offending your delicate sensibilities."

"Might, might not, I'll let you know. I saw the trailer for that last game you worked on."

"Really? Just stumbled across that, did you?"

"I had to check something in one of the rooms. It was on TV."

That trailer's only available online, no TV spots yet. She would've had to take the time to look it up. "So what'd you think?" It's normal for us to fall back into conversation like this, as if no time has passed. Normal is good. I need normal.

"You modeled the girl with the sword after me."

"You wish. I had nothing to do with that character design." It's a blatant lie, but she's being cocky again. Besides, she lied about the trailer. "Any other thoughts?"

"It looks cool. Badass. Should've had a jetpack though. Everyone wants a videogame with a jetpack"

"It's set in medieval times."

"So? You couldn't put in a jetpack as a cheat code or something? It's all just ones and zeros anyway, right?"

"I'll keep it in the idea file. How's it going over there?"

Jess swears under her breath. "The computer system, you would not believe what a clusterfuck it is. Like pulling teeth trying to set up a reservation."

"That good, huh?"

There's a pause on her end. "I was attempting to fix the clusterfuck today. Booked a room for someone with your first name."

"Yeah? Did you refer to her parents as pot smoking flower children as well?"

"You should visit sometime. I'll get you a good deal."

No smartass comeback. I'm surprised enough that I don't speak right away, and Jess rushes to fill the silence.

"When you're not up against it at work, obviously. And you really should be sleeping."

She knows I can't. If I could sleep properly, we wouldn't have met. "Right back at you, boss lady."

Jess makes a dismissive noise. "Anything specific causing it this time?"

There's a tone. I think. I want to tell her the truth.

I think she wants that. "Up against it at work, like you said."

"Right. Well. You, you overachieving nerd, must sleep. And I am going to make that happen."

"Oh really?"

"Yup. I need to go over these budget reports. You need to sleep. If listening to this crap doesn't knock you out, nothing will."

I snort back a laugh. "Multitasking again?"

"Of course. Now shut up, lie back, and let the boredom carry you off."

Smiling, I do as she says. She's right, eventually I do drift off while she talks about the cost of pillowcases and problems in accounts receivable. I fight it as long as I can, holding on to her voice.

❧❧❧❧

"You're being stupid. So stupid. You're not naturally stupid, so why are you being so stupid?"

I sigh, and then take a long sip of my drink. So much for a lunch full of comfort and emotional support. "Thank you, Emma, truly. That helps so much."

Shaking her head, Emma flags down our waitress, asks for refills on chips and salsa, and then shakes her head again when we're alone. Despite our initial frustrations with each other, Jess's roommate eventually proved to be a valued friend. I'd value her more if she'd ever bothered to develop some sort of filter, but nobody's perfect. Also, she's the only one I can really talk to about Jess.

"What do you want me to say? I've been waiting for one of you to make a move since college. Now Jess takes off, you *still* won't make a move, and you want sympathy? Oh, boo hoo. My smart, sexy, gorgeous girlfriend went away because I was too afraid to shift our relationship out of park. Poor me."

"She wasn't my girlfriend," I mutter, picking at the napkin on my lap.

"And whose fault was that? Don't get me wrong, doll. You're both being all kinds of stupid, plenty of stupid to go around, but you're right here and she's not. And again, whose fault is that?"

"What is it you expect me to do, Em? Hop a plane and tell her I accidentally fell in love with her? Beg her to choose me over her job?"

"Of course not. You should stay here; go on half-assed dates with people you don't like, and cry into your nachos. Oh wait, you're doing that already."

I take another long drink of my margarita. I tried a few times, with women who are really quite lovely. No reason I shouldn't have had a good time. Except that they weren't Jess. "Listen. This? What I'm feeling? This is exactly why we had this deal in the first place, so things wouldn't get complicated."

Emma rolls her eyes. "Please. Things were always complicated between you. You've been in love since freshmen year."

"That's not—"

"Did she not stay up half the night blabbing to you about nothing until you fell asleep? Even though she had a hundred other things that needed doing?"

I open my mouth. Start to tell her this isn't a big deal, Jess has done it countless times before. Then I realize that yes, it is a big deal, and it wouldn't exactly help my case.

"Did you not skip your final exam on Mario Kart or whatever the hell it was to take care of her when she got that stomach thing?"

Sighing, I lean back into the vinyl booth. The trip to the ER and the make-up test I had to beg for were almost as bad as the smell in my car after Jess got sick in it. I push my plate away. "Just because you left her to suffer on her own, doesn't mean I could."

"Exactly. Look. She came with me to my sister's place once, right? We're watching my nephew. He started playing his Nintendo or whatever it is he's addicted to. Playing one of your games. Jess gets all happy and bouncy. 'Skye did that. Look at that waterfall monster, that was Skye's.' On and on. It was really sweet. And annoying, which is why the kid turned off the game to play outside. You know how mushy and disgusting Jess had to get to make a nine-year-old put down a videogame?"

I don't know what to say. I stutter something else about why we did it this way, why we weren't supposed to get attached.

"You two and your divorce scars. God. Your parents fucked you up, join the club. Just do the opposite of what they did and you'll be fine."

"It's not that easy."

"You know, probably not. Who said it was supposed to be? As long as you've known me, I've been looking for the right person."

"Is that what you call it?" I ask, recalling the many, many men who'd graced Emma's side of Jess's dorm.

"Shut up. I search and search for someone I give a damn about who gives a damn about me, and nothing. You've had it for years. And you let it go because it's hard? Complicated? Because you maybe, possibly could screw it up later? Stupid. You're not stupid or lazy or cowardly, but that's how you're acting. Both of you.

Stupid, lazy, cowardly lesbians!"

Emma gets loud when she's excited. I'm not surprised that her voice raised so much near the end, that half the restaurant is now eyeing us. Half the restaurant, plus our waitress, just returned with the chips and salsa. She glances between us, coughs, then ask if we want to split the bill. Emma says she'll take care of it. That she's already given me a reality check, so it's only fair she take care of the other one too. I hide behind my margarita glass.

❧❧❧❧

I don't get nervous during flights. Usually. When I go to Reno, I spend half the journey convincing the man next to me that I'm not going to throw up on him and the other half staying stiff and silent, trying not to make myself a liar.

I spent the better part of a week digesting Emma's advice. Then there was work. My boss didn't want me gone, but I have so many vacation days racked up that he couldn't say no. All those dates I never went on when Jess was away, I had plenty of chances for overtime.

Jess's hotel is nice. Classy, but not ostentatious. My hand shakes as I pull my one piece of luggage to the front desk. Jess isn't in the lobby. I don't know if that makes things easier or harder.

Check in is, as Jess would say, a clusterfuck. I panic when I'm told there's no reservation in my name. Then I remember I registered as someone else, in case Jess was manning the computer again and saw my information. The kid behind the desk looks about the same age I was when she and I met. His expression is understandably wary; I'm acting like a crazy person.

It gets worse when I ask to speak to the manager, realizing too late that I can't just wander around the building until I see Jess. It's amazing how terrible I was at planning this. The kid tries to appease me, says he or one of the other staff members can help with anything I need. I disagree. We go like this for a few rounds. I could give him Jess's name, but I don't know what she's said or not said about me.

By the time he gets on the phone to call Jess I'm ready to puke again, and wouldn't that be a lovely welcome? I close my eyes, concentrate on breathing, and open them when I hear the ding of an elevator.

Jess is stunning. Hair as long and beautiful as I remember, dark blue skirt that's professional but sexy. The look on her face, the way her mouth drops open, it's almost enough to forget my nerves.

Things are a whirl after that. The poor kid tries to tell her that I'm being difficult. She leans in close to him, whispers low. He goes very pale and nods repeatedly. I don't catch the words, but the glint in her eyes, the way she's holding herself, it's scary. Also, hot as hell.

I start to say something, but Jess is faster. She takes my bag in one hand, urging me to follow. We go to the elevator. I can't read her face. Several floors up, the doors open on an empty hallway. Jess uses her free hand to grab mine and squeezes. She basically drags me to a door at the end of the corridor. When she has to turn the knob it's my luggage she lets go of, not me. I think she'd forget it altogether if I didn't pull it in behind us.

The door clicks shut. I get half a second to notice that the office is pretty nice but not as nice as Jess deserves. There's a large desk. She shoves me against it, and thank God because I can't stand on my own, not with what she's doing.

Our last kiss was sweet and tender. This isn't. Jess's lips are hard and desperate and everywhere. She claws at my back. I don't complain. She lifts me onto the desk and I hear things fall. Doesn't matter. I'd go on like this forever, but then I realize she's shaking. Jess is *shaking*.

I pull back, put a finger to her lips. "Hey. Hey, it's fine, okay? It's okay."

"It's not. You…what the hell are you doing here?"

Suddenly I don't want to talk. I want more of what we were doing moments ago. But talking is important. She has to know things are different now. "I fucked up." Not how I wanted to start, but it's progress. "I love you, okay? And I should've chased you through the damn airport. Because I can't be without you. I thought I could because of how it's always been, but I can't. Not really. And I don't know how to do this, any of it. The commitment thing, the long distance, but I think I can figure it out if you can. I can't figure out life without you in it. So please, don't ask me to."

Silence follows. I rushed to get the words out, now there's nothing. I'm back to not being able to read Jess. She just looks at me for the longest time, and then she doesn't. She leaves me sitting on the edge of her desk and walks around it. Half-pissed, half-panicked, I watch her sort through the mess on the floor, the stuff that fell when she manhandled me up here. "Really? Nothing? Jess, I swear to God, if you—"

She holds up a hand, comes back to me. She's holding something in her other hand. She sets it down and I have to swallow tears. It's a picture of us on graduation day, caps and gowns, all smiles, arms wrapped around each other.

"That's the most important thing in this building.

Or it was, before you showed up and gave me a stroke. I can't have it getting wrecked."

I can't speak. She pulls me into another hug, squeezing so tight it almost hurts.

"You came all the way here to tell me that?"

"Well. Didn't think Facetime would have the same impact. Also, Emma called me a stupid, cowardly lesbian, so it was kind of a pride thing."

Jess pulls away, eyes flashing. "Emma called you what?"

She's gone scary protective again and it shouldn't make me laugh. It does. I explain the conversation as quickly as I can. Jess kisses me after, swears, and then kisses me again.

"Dammit. She'll have a field day with this. Already she thinks I owe my whole career to her because if I hadn't stood up to her in college, I wouldn't have learned to stand up to these corporate assholes."

"Aren't you badmouthing your own kind there?"

"Shut up, hippie."

She leans me back further on the desk, covering my body with hers. She's careful about not jostling the picture.

"Don't know what I hate more. The fact that I do actually owe her this time, or that you got to chase after me and be all corny and romantic before I got to chase after you."

"You were going to—"

"Moot point, let's not talk about it."

It's most certainly not moot, but I let it go for now, pulling Jess closer, the strong thigh under that skirt finding a place between mine. Jess might owe Emma, but she owes me more, months, years worth of more, and I'm starting the collection process right now.

N.R. Dunham lives in Wisconsin but doesn't like beer, so it's surprising that she hasn't been kicked out of the state yet. She earned an English degree, which she uses to write articles on anything pertaining to pop culture. She's a reader, a writer, and a lover of Netflix.

Cupcakes, Art Class, and First Dates

Shannon M. Harris

Lillie carefully measured the dry ingredients, for her Grandmother's red cake recipe, into her green mixing bowl and set it aside while her sister, Casey, mumbled incoherently and flipped through the pages of the latest gossip magazine. Next she added the butter and sugar to her cranberry KitchenAid Stand Mixer, which she had named Sally, and set it on low to cream the ingredients together. When the consistency was to her liking she added the eggs, vanilla and red food coloring. She picked up the green bowl and carefully poured the dry contents into the wet ingredients in batches until everything was incorporated.

Casey stood up and leaned against the black quartz countertop. "So, L, what's been going on with you lately?"

Lillie ignored her while she sprayed her muffin pans and poured the cake batter evenly into each one. Only when she had both pans safely tucked away into the oven did she turn to face her. You couldn't tell by looking at them that they were sisters. While Casey took after their father with dark, curly locks and baby blue eyes, Lillie took after their great, great grandfather with straight, auburn hair and hazel eyes. "Quite recently I was tasked with making my nephews cupcakes for his school fundraiser." She arched her eyebrow and crossed her arms across her chest.

Casey waved her hand in the air. "I know you're the best sister a girl could ever have, and I bow down to your talents in the kitchen. Ethan and his teacher were quite happy when I told them you would be making the cupcakes." She rolled her eyes.

"You gave eleven people food poisoning last year. Good grief, I would be happy too. You know I would do anything for him." Ethan was in second grade and the light of her life.

"Don't change the subject."

She sighed and walked to the refrigerator. After pouring each of them a glass of milk she sat down at the table, followed by Casey.

"So? Is there anyone special?" Casey said, as she dipped her spoon into the cake batter and took a bite. "It tastes much better raw, than cooked."

How could she tell her sister that yes there was someone special, but she hadn't even worked up the nerve to ask her out yet? Sarah had started delivering her mail seven months ago and she hated to admit it, but she stayed home from two to five every evening just so she could catch a glimpse of her. The short talks they had every day were the highlight of her day. Sarah was friendly and very easy to talk to, and as time went on she would stay longer with each mail delivery. Her short, spiky blonde hair paired nicely with her grey eyes. It took all Lillie's self-control not to rip Sarah's uniform off every time she saw her. Those tight blue shorts showed off her backside quite nicely. She coughed and took a drink of her milk.

Casey pointed her spoon at her. "You're blushing." She stood up and deposited the bowl and spoon into the sink. "I know that look. Who is she and why haven't you told me about her?"

"Look," She stopped talking when the doorbell rang and was standing up when Casey walked out of the kitchen to the front door. The clock read twelve-twenty-three so it couldn't be Sarah. She heard talking, then laughter. She bit her lip when Casey walked back in and pointed to the door.

"You have a package you have to sign for."

"What?" Lillie stood up and her chair toppled backward. She took off her apron and smoothed her hands down her shirt. Sarah was early.

Casey grabbed her arm before she could walk past her. "Wait." She pointed to Lillie's face.

Lillie scrunched up her nose. "Let go," she growled.

"Okay." Casey put her hands up and took a step back.

Lillie took a deep breath and walked into the living room. Sarah stood just outside the door with a small package in her hand. She smiled when Lillie opened the door and walked out. The longer they stood in silence the bigger Sarah's smile became. "So," Lillie said, and pointed to the package.

Sarah shook her head. "Sorry. Just sign here." She handed over the package, and then ran her hand through her hair. "Well." She rocked back on her heels.

"You're early." Lillie stuttered.

"Am I?" Sarah grinned and Lillie felt like melting into the pavement. Stupid.

Lillie bit her lip. "From usual. Yes."

"I see." She scuffed her shoe on the sidewalk. "I was wondering if? What I mean is?" She took a deep breath. "Would you like to go to the Miller Food Convention this Saturday with me? I know it's short notice, but I gave myself a pep talk this morning, and finally worked up the nerve to ask you out."

"Yes." Lillie all but shouted. "Wait. No."

"No." Disappointed littered her voice.

Lillie grabbed her arm. "No. Yes."

"Yes."

Lillie took a deep breath and smiled. "I would love to go with you."

Sarah let out the breath she was holding and squeezed Lillie's hand. "I thought for a minute there. Never mind. Good. Okay." She nodded. "So Saturday morning. I'll pick you up around eight-thirty. The show starts at nine?"

"Saturday at eight-thirty."

Sarah backed away with one last squeeze to Lillie's hand. "I have to get back to work."

"Yes."

Lillie watched her until she got to the sidewalk and was about to go back in when Sarah turned around. "Tomorrow I'll make sure to be on time." She winked.

Lillie dropped her head, squeezed the package to her chest, and walked back into the house. Casey was sitting on the couch with her feet propped on the coffee table and had the biggest grin Lillie had ever seen on her face. She pointed her spoon at her. "She's hot."

"Whatever." Lillie frowned when she noticed Sarah was eating the frosting for the cupcakes, but was on such a high she didn't say anything to her.

"She really likes you."

"You think?"

"I do." She nodded and took another bite.

Lillie sat down across from her and frowned. There was always that nagging thought that it wouldn't turn out to be anything serious. She didn't want to imagine the day Sarah stopped delivering her mail. "How can you be so sure?"

"Well, for one thing, that's an empty box." She pointed to the box in Lillie's arms.

Lillie looked down and noticed for the first time there wasn't any address written on it. She opened it to be sure and Casey was right, it was empty. She grinned and threw it on the coffee table. "And?"

"You have cake batter smeared across your face."

"What?" She jumped up and looked in the mirror that hung by the front door. Sure enough, there was cake batter smeared across her nose and down her cheek. She went to the kitchen, washed her face, then marched back to the couch and yanked the bowl out of her sister's hand. "Why didn't you tell me?"

"I did, but you were like grrr, don't touch me and grrr, back off. So I did." She shrugged. "What does it matter? She was probably thinking about licking it off of you anyway. See?" She pointed her finger at Lillie. "You were thinking it too."

"Whatever." She sat down and looked at the bowl in her hands then at her sister. Something wasn't right. Casey never ate this much sweet stuff. "What's going on with you? How's Rebecca?"

Casey swung her legs up and lay back on the couch. "I went to surprise her at home last week and I caught her fucking little Miss Choir herself, Bethany Meyer."

"Shut up. Miss better-than-you?"

Casey rose up on her arm. "Yes, and if my girlfriend hadn't been between her legs I would have thought it was funny." She flopped back on the couch.

Lillie knew break ups were hard and even worse when you were cheated on, but to her knowledge Casey and Rebecca were mostly casual. They only went out a couple of times a month. She'd only introduced her to

Ethan once and that was by accident.

"What's that looking for?" Casey said.

"Well. Ethan and I didn't like her to begin with."

"What?" She sat up. "Why didn't either of you say anything? You're supposed to have my back."

"It's hard to have your back when Rebecca had your front. I get it. She cheated on you, but be truthful, you weren't all that serious about her to begin with."

"Whatever." Casey flopped back on the couch.

"You know what? Tonight." It had been a while since they had been out together. It was time to change that.

"Tonight?"

"We're going out tonight. You and me. Mom and dad will watch Ethan. Be here at six. I know just the place."

Casey pushed up from the couch, grabbed the bowl from Lillie's hand and took another bite of the frosting. "Six."

❧ ❧ ❧ ❧

"L, this isn't exactly what I had in mind when you said we were going out."

Lillie settled into her seat and set her charcoal pencils onto the lip of the desk. Four other women, besides her and Casey, along with six men filled the small art studio. A foot-high platform stood at the front of the classroom, awaiting the model to come out, and pose atop it. Lillie had never been to a nude class before, but she had been to quite a few of the other art classes the art studio provided. "We were lucky to get into this class. The only reason we did was because a mother and daughter had to cancel."

Casey eyed her setup. "Have you done this before?"

"Not this particular class, but I have been to quite a few of the other ones."

"All right, class," a woman at the front of the class said. "My name is Beatrice and I will be your teacher for this evening. I am here to help you in any way I can. Don't hesitate to ask questions. I see some familiar faces and some new ones. I am sure everyone in this room has seen a naked body before. Keep that in mind when the model comes out. We are all adults here."

"Lillie," Casey whispered. "Is the model a man or a woman?" She unwrapped a sucker and popped it in her mouth.

Lillie rolled her eyes. "A woman, I believe. I thought it would get your mind off of what's-her-name."

"Good thinking."

"I thought so." Lillie shut up and her eyes widened when the model walked out in a robe. "Casey." She pinched her arm.

"What?"

"Look at the model." This couldn't be happening. Not now.

"Oh my god." Casey laughed. "What are the odds of that? You better look, she's getting ready to take off her robe."

Lillie's heart was in her throat and she kept her eyes glued to the paper. After a few seconds, she garnered the courage, raised her head, and locked eyes with Sarah. Sarah's eyes widened for a moment then her face settled into a mask and she turned her head away. Lillie dropped her eyes and noticed her defined shoulders first. She licked her lips and let her eyes travel farther down. The soft curve of Sarah's breast's came into view, followed by an impossibly toned and flat stomach. Blond curls, and toned thighs and calves followed rounded hips. She was exquisite and Lillie was, at the moment, intimidated. She obviously took very good care of herself and all Lillie could think was that she shouldn't have eaten those two cupcakes yesterday.

Casey leaned in close to her. "She is hot." She fanned her face. "Good grief. Maybe this wasn't such a good idea after all." She laughed and focused on her paper.

Maybe it wasn't. But, one of her questions had been answered; Sarah was a natural blond. With each glide of her pencil her heart rate settled and she got lost in the act of drawing. She was so lost in the moment that she didn't realize Beatrice was standing beside her.

"Very good. Your shading is remarkable." She pointed at Lillie's paper. "And." She turned to Casey. "Keep practicing, dear. You'll get there."

Lillie glanced at Casey's sketch and snickered. "Going for abstract, were you?"

"Well," Casey said. "Not intentionally, no, but you shouldn't fight what comes naturally. Should you?"

After Beatrice walked around and checked everyone's drawings, she walked to the front of the class. "All right, everyone. That's a wrap." She handed Sarah her robe and she slipped it on. Lillie felt a twinge of disappointment when Sarah walked out of the classroom. "Everyone can pack up their things. It's been a good class."

"Lillie," Casey said. "That's really good." She picked up her piece of paper. "How long have you been taking classes?"

Lillie shrugged and picked up her bag. "Couple of years."

"What? And this is the first I'm hearing about

this. What am I saying? Of course you're good at this. You're good at everything you do."

"Don't be so hateful. You're still mom and dad's favorite."

"I know. Ethan was my saving grace."

Lillie laughed and took the paper out of her hand, and rolled it up. When she slipped it into her bag she noticed Sarah had walked back into the room. She had on a pair of blue jeans and a long sleeved, white Henley.

"Go talk to her." Casey patted her arm.

With each step to the front of the classroom her heart rate tripled. She stood back while Sarah and Beatrice talked and couldn't help but smile when Sarah walked up to her.

"So," Sarah said, and ran her fingers through her hair. "Did you enjoy class?" She bit her lip.

"I will admit, it was different than the one's I usually take, but it was very informative."

She laughed. "I bet. It was a bit of a shock when I saw you sitting at one of the desks, but." She shrugged. "You would have seen me naked sooner or later."

"Yay." Lillie scoffed her foot along the floor. "After the initial shock of seeing you, and a moment to admire you, I focused on the drawing."

"As it should be. Look. Since you're here, do you want to, maybe, go get some ice cream or something?"

Lillie fought the urge to jump up and down. She was an adult after all. "Ice cream sounds good." Lillie swung her head around when Casey wrapped her arms around her.

"I don't mean to interrupt you, but Lillie, you're my ride home."

Lillie frowned. "I am her ride."

Sarah pushed her hands into her pockets. "That's

not a problem. Lillie, I can take you home."

"That's settled then." Lillie pulled her keys out of her pocket and handed them to Casey.

Casey eyed the keys then Lillie. "Are you sure, L? You never let me drive your car."

Lillie waved her off. "It's fine. I know you'll take good care of her."

"If you're sure?" She sang.

"I am."

"Well then. Sarah, it was nice to see you again. And, ladies, don't do anything I wouldn't do." She winked and skipped out of the classroom.

"So," Sarah said. "You ready?"

"I am."

❧ ❧ ❧ ❧

Lillie settled onto the top of the picnic table beside Sarah and looked out over the water. After getting their ice cream they decided it would be a nice night to go to the park and eat it. Lillie took a lick of hers and savored the delicate mint undertones that complimented the chocolate. It was the first date she had had in a long time and she felt so comfortable with Sarah. Sarah didn't feel like a stranger and in her experience that was a new feeling.

"Do you want a bite?" Sarah asked.

"It's vanilla. Shouldn't I be asking if you want a bite of mine?"

Sarah laughed and leaned back on the tabletop. "It's a beautiful night. A perfect date night."

"It is." She wasn't sure what to say. Every time words would come she would get a lump in her throat and she choked them back. She didn't want to say the *wrong* thing. She didn't want to blow this.

"Do you know what I want?" Sarah said out of the blue. "I want to meet someone and plan a life together. Maybe have a few kids. I want to make plans and live out our dreams together. I can't wait to hold hands, in our matching rocking chairs that we bought from Cracker Barrel, when we get old. I want someone that wants those things too. Someone that just doesn't want to date, but someone who wants a life together. I don't want casual."

"That sounds amazing," Lillie said, and fumbled with the empty bowl in her hands. It sounded too good to be true. "Everything except the rocking chairs. I mean who can really afford the ones from Cracker Barrel. Probably have to get them at a yard sale."

Sarah laughed and reached for her bowl. "Give me your bowl. I am going to throw these away and if you want we can walk closer to the water.

"Sounds good." She pushed off the table and walked to the edge of the hill that overlooked the river. She sighed when Sarah wrapped her arms around her, tensed for a moment, and then relaxed back into the arms that held her. This certainly wasn't what she had planned for tonight. Nowhere near what she had planned.

"It's funny," Sarah said. "I have been waiting for this for months, and now that we're here I don't know exactly what to say."

Lillie knew that feeling. "I don't either, but the silence doesn't bother me. I'm comfortable just spending time with you."

"That's not right," Sarah said and Lillie frowned. "It's not that I don't know what to say it's just that I don't want to scare you off with what I do have to say."

Lillie turned around slowly so that they were facing each other. Sarah looked way more serious than she should have on a first date. She wasn't sure if she wanted to hear what she had to say or not. "It's just a first date. No pressure. Let's see where this goes." She fiddled with the buttons on her shirt.

Sarah stepped back and ran her hands through her hair. "That's just it. I know where this goes." She grasped Lillie's hands between hers and took several deep breaths. "Lillie."

"Wait," Lillie said, afraid of what came next. Her heart felt like it would beat out of her chest.

Sarah shook her head. "No. I can't wait. Lillie, I am in love with you."

Lillie pulled her hands away and took several steps backward. She couldn't have heard what she thought she had. "You can't be serious. Are you crazy?" She had to be crazy. That was the only explanation. How did she always get stuck with the crazy ones? "We don't even know each other. You can't be in love with me. You don't know anything about me." Lillie gulped at the look on Sarah's face.

Sarah shook her head. "Lillie. I know what your favorite color is and your favorite food. I know that you're having trouble finishing the third book in the series you're writing. I know all about your love of baking and your love for naming your appliances. I know how much you hurt when your father had a heart attack and how grateful you were when he came home from the hospital. I can name all your favorite aunts and uncles and I know that you would give anything to spend just one more minute with your grandma. I've seen you with makeup on and without it. I've seen you dressed up and with a pair of cut off sweatpants on and a t-shirt that has seen better days. And I know you love to garden, but it doesn't always love you." Sarah picked up Lillie's hand and placed it above her heart. "Lillie, we've been dating for months and you didn't even realize it. The first time I walked up your drive to deliver your mail my heart literally stopped beating when you walked out of our house and looked at me. I was so tongue tied and kept fumbling with your mail in my hands and I tried to think of something clever and witty to say, but you kept looking at your watch. When I got a few houses down I finally remembered to breathe."

Lillie shook her head. She remembered that day as if it were yesterday. It was the day that changed her life and her outlook of it. "I kept looking at my watch because I wanted to remember what time it was, so that I knew what time you would be by the next day, and the next. I purposely stayed home between two and five every day so that I wouldn't miss an opportunity to see and talk to you."

"See." Sarah smiled. "Your head may not know it, but your heart does. Please, don't fight it. These types of feelings don't come around very often. Please give us the chance we deserve."

Lillie turned toward the water and blew on her fingers. Everything was happening to soon. Too fast. Real life didn't happen like this. This was the stuff of fantasies and the stories that she wrote. That Sarah would choose her was...this wasn't in her plans. Not like this. You didn't just jump into these things. There should be months of planning and talking and dating. I love you's didn't come when you were eating ice cream on your first date. She bit her lip. Or did they? For goodness sake, they hadn't even kissed yet.

"Lillie, stop overthinking this. I know I haven't

misread the signs and I can understand your reluctance. I'm not asking to move in with you, or even asking you to marry me. Those things will come later. But, Lillie, look at me. I am in love with you and I don't think that's a bad place for us to start from. Do you?"

"This stuff never happens to me. I am never someone's first choice."

"You were mine."

"Why do you have to say everything so right? You're perfect and I'm flawed. Why me?"

"Stop. You're not flawed. You're perfect, and trust me, I have my issues. I don't like cheese and I don't enjoy reality television. I have issues with road rage and even though I am mail carrier, I think the postal system is flawed. I don't enjoy swimming and I can't, for the life of me, understand how someone can spend half their life messing with their phone."

Lillie blew out the breath she was holding and waved her hands in the air. "I know all of those things." She shut her mouth when Sarah grinned at her and rocked back on her heels. Oh my god! She did know all of those things about her and she also knew her favorite meal was chicken and dumplings and she loved broccoli. She had a wiener dog named Harry and a pet guinea pig named Pig. She closed her eyes and didn't resist when Sarah embraced her. Over the last seven months they had been getting to know each other one minute at a time. She closed her eyes and enjoyed being wrapped in Sarah's arms. Falling in love didn't happen on the first date, but this wasn't their first date. The shift had been so subtle she hadn't even noticed.

"I don't think this is a bad place to start," Sarah said. "In the coming months we will learn plenty more about each other. There will be fights and disagreements, but there will also be love. It takes work, but I am willing and ready to give us everything we need to succeed. Are you?"

Lillie raised her head and looked into her eyes and didn't fight the feelings that overwhelmed her. Meeting Sarah for the first time felt like a lifetime ago and in a way it was. The peace she felt now, wrapped in her arms, felt too right not to be real. What had Casey said? You shouldn't fight what comes naturally. So she didn't. "Kiss me."

Born near Chicago, IL, but raised in Southern Illinois, Shannon is a diehard Whovian and enjoys anything having to do with Science Fiction and Fantasy. In her free time, when she isn't writing, she enjoys binge watching true crime shows. She lives in the country with her three fur kids.

Secret Admirer

Tara Wentz

Day after day I watched her. I wondered more than once if she were aware of curious eyes upon her body. I've lost count of the number of times her scent, carried by the air around her, has enveloped my senses. My fingers begging to touch her long, shiny, dark locks…so close, yet so far away. Those brown eyes looking at me as though they could see right through any façade I could possibly hide behind. Not that I would want to, but you understand the point I'm trying to make, don't you? It wasn't that I was stalking her or anything, more like we happened to be in the same places…and quite often at that.

I suppose now would be a good time to tell you that not only do I work with this woman, but I also live in the same building. Her name is Kiplan and I've been in love with her as long as I've known her. Of course, she's not exactly aware that I have these feelings for her, I mean, how could I possibly tell her?

You see, it all started out innocent enough. After I moved into the building we became fast friends. We'd go out to eat on occasions, watch movies together, and do laundry at the same time…got the picture? When she became jobless because of the downsizing of the company she worked for I informed her of the openings at my firm. I even went to bat for her when they needed a character reference. That was almost two years ago. I knew then how I felt about her, and I also knew nothing could ever come of it. She'd never had a steady girlfriend, but she'd had plenty of dates with some very attractive women. Based on the women coming and going from her apartment, she was definitely out of my league.

Saturday night seemed to change everything. We were eating Chinese food and watching one of those documentaries on the aftermath of Hurricane Katrina. The anger and sadness coming from the victims was overwhelming. At one point I looked over and Kiplan had tears running down her cheeks. I sat my food down, grabbed a Kleenex, and leaned over to dry her tears. I cupped her cheek and dabbed gently. She smiled and that stopped me in my tracks. We stared at each other for the longest time. Just as she was about to say something I got scared. I jumped up and took my plate to the kitchen and told her I needed to go. I could tell she didn't want me to leave and that alone gave me hope…or at least I should say the desire to try and let her know how I felt.

Today I'm not running. Still scared, but no more running.

"Hunter?"

"Hunter!"

I jerked from my musings and blinked my eyes. "What?"

The object of my desire was standing so close I could feel the heat coming off her body.

"I wanted to know if you'd be available to go over these spreadsheets tonight. I'm cutting out in a bit to run an errand."

"Sure. Yeah, I'll be home, just give me a holler when you're ready."

"Okay. I'll talk to you later then," Kiplan replied

with a smile.

I glanced at my watch, knowing that Manny would be here any minute. The dinging of the elevator drew my attention. Twelve-year-old Manny Gonzalez walked through the open elevator doors with the delivery in his hands. He caught my eye and smiled knowingly before heading towards Kiplan's desk. I watched curiously as he approached and held his hands out to her.

That smile I absolutely adored lit her face as she took the two perfect yellow roses from him and sniffed them appreciatively. She talked to him for a minute before laughing out loud. I couldn't hear a word she was saying, but the smile said it all. As he turned to leave she grabbed his arm. I saw her lean closer and whisper something to him. He smiled a big toothy grin at her, took something from her hand and headed back in my direction. He didn't stop, but merely nodded and kept on his way.

Going over the spreadsheets with her tonight about drove me insane. She smelled so good and seemed to take every opportunity to touch me. A caress on my arm to get my attention. Her nails running lightly across my back as she crossed behind me. Her fingers sifting through my hair when I announced I needed a haircut. I mean, a gal can only take so much.

"Son of a bitch!" I groaned and rolled over trying everything I knew to get to sleep. Just thinking about her made my body throb. There was only one way to release the tension enough so I could maybe get some sleep before the alarm went off. I reached down and slid my hand beneath the soft cotton of my boxers and sighed.

Tuesday had Manny arriving with three yellow roses. Wednesday brought four yellow roses. Thursday was two more yellow roses. Friday was a single red rose in full bloom and a note card attached. Each time Manny delivered the flowers he would spend a few minutes talking to Kiplan before leaving. And on his way out he'd nod in my direction.

I stood and walked over to Kiplan's desk. She was busy arranging the last rose within the vase of the yellow ones.

"Secret admirer?" I asked.

She sniffed the newest flower before claiming her seat. "It looks that way. Aren't they gorgeous?"

"Yes, they certainly are." *But not near as gorgeous as you.*

"And this time there was a card attached," Kiplan replied, handing it over.

I didn't really need to see the card to know what it said since I was the one who wrote it, but I had to play this out to the end so I read it quietly and handed it back.

"So, a date, huh? Are you going to go?"

"Mmmm, I'm not sure. I mean, what exactly do I know about this person anyhow?"

Fuck!

"Well, maybe you should give it a chance. It might be worth your time."

Right now all I wanted to do was get the hell out of there before she had time to say anything more.

"Yeah, maybe so. I suppose if this person shows up and I'm not the least bit interested I could always have you intervene, huh?"

"Well, there is that, yes," I said, silently triumphing. Now I just hoped that she wouldn't be disappointed with the outcome.

I stood before the long mirror on the back of my bedroom door and appraised my outfit. Black slacks with matching black shoes that were polished to a shine.

A royal blue button-down silk shirt neatly tucked and topped with a black belt. The hue of the shirt brought out the blue in my eyes or so I was told. My straight dishwater blonde hair brushed at least 100 times making it soft and smooth.

This is it Hunter. Tonight's the night.

I knocked gently on the door and waited. When no one answered I knocked again, a little louder this time. Still no answer so I tried the knob. To my surprise the door was unlocked.

I poked my head in and glanced around. The lights in the living room were dimmed and music was softly playing on the stereo.

"I'm in the kitchen, Hunter."

How did she know it was I? It could have been anybody! I walked around the corner and stopped dead in my tracks. Kiplan was standing with her back against the counter, holding two glasses of wine. She was wearing an off the shoulder bright red dress with come-fuck-me black stiletto heels. Her hair was a mass of dark curls falling over her bare shoulders. She smiled and stepped forward.

"H—," I started, but she placed two fingers over my lips.

"How did I know it was you?" At my nod she continued. "Your little partner in crime turned rogue the very first day. He told me that you paid him 5 dollars each day to deliver the roses to me."

"Figures," I replied, shaking my head.

"It's about time, ya know? A girl can only wait so long."

I stared at her for a brief moment before making a decision I knew would either haunt me forever or make me the happiest woman alive. I took a sip of wine, sat the glass on the table, and then stepped closer to her. She took one final step to close the distance between us and I wrapped my arms around her waist. I pulled her firmly against me and lowered my head, claiming her lips. I kissed her until I couldn't breathe. Pulling away, I gasped for air before she pulled me back against her.

"I want you, Hunter," she rasped into my ear.

I took her lips again with lightning speed. I couldn't get enough of her. My lips nipped at hers before traveling down her neck. The skin was so soft. I bit gently at her shoulder as I walked her backwards to the counter and eased her onto it. She tore open the front of my shirt sending buttons flying everywhere. I couldn't have cared less that my new forty-dollar shirt was now ruined. I tossed the offending garment to the side and reached behind her to unzip her dress. It dropped to her waist, but I didn't notice. My eyes were glued to her perfect breasts encased in red lace. My mouth went dry and my hands were shaking as I reached up to unclasp the strapless number. I dropped it on the floor with my shirt and took her in my hands. Leaning forward I buried my face between her breasts and took a deep breath.

"Please, Hunter."

My tongue traced around one nipple while my fingers squeezed and kneaded the other. She leaned back against the cabinets that pushed her hips closer to me. I could smell how excited she was which only fueled me further. My hands dropped to her hips and pulled at the dress. She wriggled her hips side to side until the dress was shimmied up around her waist. Again that damn red lace mocked me, but I was not deterred. With help, I slid the panties down and off her legs. She was gorgeous… absolutely stunning. Her skin was flushed with arousal and her eyes were ablaze with heat.

"Are you absolutely sure this is what you want, Kip?"

"If you don't shut up and finish what you started I won't be held responsible for my actions."

I chuckled and then gasped as she wrapped her legs around me and her stiletto's dug into the back of my thighs. I squeezed her hips with my hands and kissed her again. Slowly I worked my way down her body and bit the inside of her thigh, none too gently.

"Oh!" I heard her exclaim and she opened her legs even wider.

I nuzzled the skin on her thigh as I worked my way to the apex between her legs. My thumbs opened her wide as I took one long lick before I settled on her clit. Her hands pulled my head closer while my tongue fluttered across her. I knew she was getting close. Her hips were moving in time with my mouth and I could hear her laboring for each breath. I slid two fingers inside her and her clit immediately hardened.

"I'm coming, Hunter…Oh, God!"

Her orgasm flooded over my fingers. She trembled and all I wanted to do was hold her close to me. Slowly I removed my fingers and wrapped my arms around her. I pulled her against my chest and held her.

Now you're wondering what happened, right? Well, let's just say that I was never haunted, but I did move out of the building. I also got a promotion at work and was asked to head another department. That was all fine with me because it made things much easier on Kip. I wouldn't want anyone thinking I was giving my wife preferential treatment. We bought a beautiful two story Victorian house and are working on the renovations. As for Manny, well he was worth far more than the five dollars a visit I paid him, even if he did turn against me. I found out later that Kip paid him five dollars every visit as well…the little con artist.

Tara lives in Missouri with her wife and has been in the medical field for over 25 years. When not working or writing, Tara likes to read, dabble with photography and watch sports. She has two novels, Traffic Stop and Deception by Design and is currently at work on her third.

Website: www.tarawentz.com

Sweetest Truth

S.Y. Thompson

I'm not good at romance, never have been. Emotions are as foreign to me as some of the worlds I visited in the name of human expansion. Somehow, my captain has managed to find the chink in my armor. I try desperately not to show it, but I think I've been less than successful.

"What do you say, Commander?"

I barely hear the question, too lost in eyes the color of sable. The gentle soul hidden within is clear to me without words. I see her hair's luster beneath the artificial glow of overhead lights and shiver at the timber of her voice. There was a time when someone might have accused me of being a romantic. Thankfully, my reputation precludes any possibility of that now.

"How…?"

"Excuse me?"

Captain Serena Powell seems entirely confused by my awkward question. I want to chicken out, to pretend I only mean to inquire about the upcoming mission. Then again, I've never been a coward. It's now or never.

I stand up from the chair in front of her desk and pull down the hem of my jacket. That small, almost habitual movement helps to center my determination. I lock my gaze with that of my captain and start around her desk. Captain Powell's eyes widen in shock and she drops the data pad. It careens off her desk and spins unheeded to the floor.

"What are you doing?"

She sounds breathless, but not frightened. If anything, I'd bet a month's credits that she is aroused. My legs tremble in fear, not of an attack, but of a rejection. Emotions are far more frightening than any battle.

Captain Powell turns her chair to the side to face me directly. I have no way of knowing whether she intends the maneuver to block my advance or to welcome me. I simply must take the chance. With that in mind, I drop to one knee in front of her.

"I think you know."

I keep my voice gentle to prevent startling her and raise a hand to cup her cheek. She gasps when my palm makes contact with the soft, warm flesh. For the briefest of moments, Captain Powell leans into the caress. Her eyes flit closed for a fraction of second before she suddenly pulls away.

"Commander Chase, this is highly inappropriate. You should return to your seat so that we can get on with this briefing."

"Or I should just kiss you."

"Are you out of your mind? Have you contracted some kind of mind altering parasite when you were on Nova One?"

I can see how she'd think that. My team and I have just returned from the newly terra-formed planet after overseeing the installation of air scrubbers. We were pulled away for a dangerous assignment into the Horsehead Nebula. The Grimlax are on the move again and war looms ever present on the horizon.

"I don't think so. Honestly, I've always had feelings for you but I've never felt so compelled to express them before."

Her throat moves as she swallows nervously. I've never seen anything so supple or utterly erotic. I can't tear my gaze away from the sight. Before I know it, I lean in close enough to feel her breath on my lips. By opening my mouth, I welcome her taste into my body.

"Do you need me to call someone?" Her words are a bare whisper, spoken with equal measures arousal and concern.

"If you call someone, I can't do this."

Finally, after countless months of want, I close the distance that separates us. My lips tease hers gently, just a stroke. Then again. Her tongue darts out to touch my upper lip and then she opens to me. I lose myself in a kiss I've dared never dream of. Our tongues tangle as electricity sings in my blood. My fingers wind into her auburn hair, pulling her to me in urgent need.

Powell responds and the kiss grows almost harsh. Hovering over me in her chair, she has the advantage of leverage. Captain Powell utilizes that leverage, bending me backward as she presses forward. Her hands grip my shoulders before sliding down and pulling my body toward her.

As quickly as the interlude began, it ends. Captain Powell shoves me away and lurches from her chair. Even as I land on my back, she steps over me. Powell strides to the other side of her office where the deck rises into a formal sitting area. A transparent gallium table rests in front of a sofa and she quickly places the furniture between us.

"I'm not sure what just happened, but it can never happen again. Do you understand, Commander?"

She emphasizes my rank as though it would impress her point upon me. She fails miserably. I could no more turn away from this than a moth disregards the flame. Alien virus or not, though I seriously doubt it, I might not get another chance.

"No, Captain Powell…Serena. You know as well as I do that this is one mission that might see the end of me. Of my entire team, for that matter."

"So you thought you'd get in an attempt to bed me before you go? You forget that I know your reputation, Commander Chase. I'm not that easy."

"First off, I don't need subterfuge to get a date. If all I wanted was sex, I'd tell you that up front."

She frowns and her brow furrows in the cutest way. "Then why? You have to know that I can't allow this."

"Because I love you. I have since the first time I saw you. I won't be like others in my command, regretting that they didn't say the words until it was too late. The war has already taken so many lives and I'm not delusional. I want you to know the truth."

I cross the deck, taking slow deliberate steps, encouraged by the fact that she doesn't run. As I climb the few steps to the upper level, I can see the pulse pounding in her throat. I want to taste that point, to suck on the tender flesh. She must have seen that desire in my eyes because she takes a step back, halted by the hull behind her.

"Stop, please."

Instead, I continue to move forward until our uniforms touch. I can feel her breasts rise and fall.

"Do you really want me to? Be honest."

"Yes. No. I…I don't know."

I want her to want me, to show that she needs this as much as I do. I brace both hands against the wall on either side of her face and lean in again. She has plenty of room to move away if that is what she wants. Instead, Serena rests her hands on my waist. Close enough.

Our lips meet again, this time without restraint. I lose myself in her taste. The sweetness of her perfume invades my nostrils and fills my lungs. Somehow, my jacket vanishes and I realize she is undressing me. Never one to be left behind, I reciprocate. Before I know it, I've divested her of the regulation jacket, tie and starched white shirt. Her bra stands out stark against tanned flesh. We stumble over to the sofa and crash down with me lying atop her.

Talented fingers release my bra with a simple twist. My breasts bounce free and Serena swiftly attacks, pinching a nipple between her finger and thumb. Moisture floods from my body and I can't help grinding into her thigh, desperate for relief.

I tear my mouth free of hers and bite down upon the pulse point that I'd found so distracting before. Serena arches into me and I feel fingernails dig into my back. I've never considered she'd be so passionate, this woman who is also so self-contained in public.

"What if someone comes in?"

"They'd never dream of it." I licked the place where my teeth had left a mark. "No one comes in unless invited."

Duty flees from my mind as her hand slides down the front of my trousers. Fingers stroke and cause me to shudder. I can't keep my eyes open and don't try. Instead, I rest my forehead against her shoulder, trembling as she teases me. When she positions her thumb at my opening, I freeze. This is the moment of no return and we both know it.

"Captain Powell to the bridge. Incoming communiqué from High Councilman Horatio."

Serena's body tenses and she jerks her hand free. The hail over the ship's intercom is like a dash of cold water. She tries to get up, but I press down more firmly. Serena frowns at me, but stops resisting.

"Tell him I'm busy at the moment, but will call him back, Lieutenant."

"Understood."

Once Serena cuts the transmission, she glares at me. I grin in return, thinking she'll be disappointed if she thinks that works on me.

"I still have a job to do."

"I know and no one does it better. Don't get all huffy, though you are cute when you pout."

"I'm a starship captain, I do not pout."

I kiss her quickly and pull away. "You do, actually."

Strong arms slide around my neck and hug me close. I feel melded to her, two beings made into one. I feel whole. In this instant, I know she feels as I do.

Serena rests her chin against my shoulder and I feel her intake of breath. She wants to talk.

"Could you ever love someone else, say if something happened to me?"

Fear causes adrenaline to replace the sting of desire. Serena has also visited the newly acquired planet. Unforeseen outbreaks are common with colonization and I worry she's contracted an alien pathogen. I pull back slightly to gauge her expression.

"Are you all right?"

She smiles and kisses the tip of my nose. "I'm fine, merely curious. As I've said, I know about your reputation."

"Sex is one thing, this is something else." I shake my head, searching for the words to help her understand. "My heart doesn't work that way. I could never love another. There's room inside for only one. That place is taken."

"You say the sweetest things."

"It's the truth. Unfortunately, duty calls and you should call the Councilman back. Just do me a favor after I leave?"

"Anything."

"Can you pick up my bra so the crew doesn't find it?"

Serena chuckles and her eyes sparkle in that fascinating way that so enchants me. "Why would you leave it here?"

"You need something to remember me by while I'm gone."

Gentle fingers stroke my cheek and Serena's hand drifts to the back of my head. "I don't think you have to worry about me forgetting. Just bring yourself home in one piece so we can pick up where we left off. That's an order, Commander."

"One I'm happy to obey."

S.Y. Thompson lives in North Texas with her Yorkie and three cats. Her previous fan fiction works can be found on her website: SYThompson.com. Susan spent ten years as a United States Marine before becoming a San Diego County Deputy Sheriff. After an early retirement, she moved back to Texas. She began publishing in 2012. She can be reached at trek7th@yahoo.com

She's Got Me
BL Clark

S nuggle in honey and close your eyes. I got you." I hear her say softly as she pulls my body to hers. I loved being in her arms. It was the one place that I felt safe and secure, as if nothing bad could happen to me. And after one of my all too frequent nightmares, that is exactly what I needed. Feeling her arms holding me tight against her body, I knew that I was loved for me, not for who I was, not for what I could do for her, but just for me. I'm not sure if you have ever had that, but when you feel it, there is nothing in this world that can compare to true, unconditional, complete love. I feel her lips pressed against the top of my head. Again, the feeling of complete love washes over me.

I know that I am lucky and that most people don't find someone who they can call their soul mate. Hell, I used to scoff at the idea that there was a perfect person for everyone out there. That was until I found Sydney. I didn't realize it, though, not at first at least. Love and romance they aren't something that I was well versed in. Yes, I had been in a few relationship, been in what I thought was love a couple of times even. But Sydney, she turned my world upside down.

Sydney and I met online. I know what you are thinking; it wasn't a matchmaking site or anything like that. No, we met during a heated discussion between book clubs regarding a book that we both loved. Sounds weird, but the book was a written in the 1950's and people were trying to apply today's principles and logic to it. That doesn't work in case you were wondering. Sydney and I were posting like views and she sent me an instant message, and we started chatting from there. What started as a few minutes here and there turned into long hours discussing books, reading, writing, and then moving to life. She became a best friend to me when I didn't realize that I needed one.

Sydney and I didn't live too far apart; we were both in the United States at least. But we were both in relationships and neither of us thought our partner's would approve of us doing more than chatting online. Hell, we even chose to not exchange pictures. Yes, I know it is odd that we didn't exchange pictures, but we felt that would take it to a level that we weren't ready for. Sydney did tell me what she looked like and I described myself. Okay, maybe we had talked a couple of times online, but really, it wasn't more than a few minutes at a time. Plus, she was happy in her relationship, mine wasn't ideal, but it worked. It wasn't until my job brought us face to face that things changed.

I make my living writing. I write books, blogs, and freelance magazine articles. I'm not picky, I just love writing. I've developed an extensive portfolio of work, which has brought me some awards and press. I have to say, the awards are nice and a bit of an ego boost, but being in front of people, or being stalked into the bathroom by an overly aggressive reporter looking for an interview, not my thing. It has happened, but thankfully only a handful of times.

Anyway, I was doing research for my latest book, and I had to travel from the East coast to the Midwest. Little did I know that this trip was going to change the course of my whole life? I arrived at the airport and got my rental car. I used the navigator on my phone to find my hotel. Once I got checked in, I decided to go out and explore the town, see what there was to do. I stopped at the front desk, and they gave me a couple of maps and directions to some of the local tourist attractions and a few of the local independent bookstores.

As I walked around enjoying the sights and sounds, I couldn't help but feeling like I knew this place. I didn't know why, but it just had a comfortable familiar feel to it. I checked out the local shops and went to the first independent bookstore. It was called Time Books. As I wandered around the store, I saw that it was a bit eclectic and had an aged feel to it.

"May I help you," asked the woman who looked like a former librarian. She had gray hair, plastic-rimmed glasses, and the crotched shall. I fought long and hard not to laugh.

"No, I was just looking." I didn't want to say, 'hey, I'm just here to see if you carry any of my books' without already knowing the answer. Asking that at times puts the shop owners on the spot. I found out the hard way that not all of them respond pleasantly.

The woman nodded and appeared to be watching me while she straightened the books. I'm not sure why she was watching me so closely. I'm not one of those dodgy looking people. Or, at least I don't see myself that way. I mean I'm five foot eight, I have short brown hair, green eyes, and I wear wire-rimmed glasses. I was wearing a pair of faded blue jeans and a green hoodie that showed off my eyes.

I looked around the store for a few more minutes before smiling at the older woman and exiting. I didn't get to look at everything I wanted to, but the old lady watching me was making me uncomfortable. I have never worked in retail, but I don't believe that is how you build a customer base.

I looked at my watch and realized it was starting to get late. I decided to head toward the hotel again. When I got back, I ordered room service and set up my computer. Logging on, I saw that I had a message from Sydney, which made me smile and totally forget about the creepy bookstore lady. Syd's message was letting me know that her partner was going to be out of town for a few days so we could actually talk on the phone. I messaged her back telling her I was out of town, but I'd be back home before her partner got back. I wasn't thinking that this trip would take too long.

After eating, I decided that the jet lag and hour time difference were enough for me to justify shutting down the computer and reading on my tablet. I knew it wouldn't be long before I was asleep.

When I woke the next morning, my face was stuck to the screen of my tablet. Yes, I had fallen asleep while reading. At least I was alone. My partner had seen me do this numerous times and rarely let me live it down. After unsticking my face from the tablet, I ordered some coffee and went to wash my face. Today I had a couple of business meetings and then I was looking forward to checking out the other two bookstores the girl at the front desk had recommended. The one she said was her favorite was the one that I was most looking forward to visiting. It had a quirky and clever name to it. Plot Twists, it just hit me as a really good name for a bookstore.

Both of my meetings went well. Having been very well prepared, there was very little that I learned in the meetings. I went back to the hotel to change and then head out to explore some more.

As I pulled up outside Plot Twists, I couldn't help but smile. The sign was a giant book with the store name on the pages and a tiny rainbow in the lower corner of one of the pages. I walked in the front door and instantly felt comfortable. The mahogany shelves gave it a rich feel, the pops of color on the signs defining each area was welcoming and not overbearing. As I wandered up and down the aisles I couldn't help but think back to the previous night and the first bookstore I was in. Night and day, worlds apart in feeling.

I came up to the Lesbian Fiction section. It was considerably larger than I had found in most of the bookstores I have been in over the years. There was a younger woman stocking the shelves, so I tried to move around her and the cart.

"Sorry," I said, as I failed to clear the cart while reaching for one of my early books.

"Oh, it's okay. These darn carts don't leave much room to maneuver around." She stood and turned to look at me then at the book in my hands. "That is a great boo…k."

"Yes, it is one of my favorites," I said, trying to play down who I was, but I could tell that this girl recognized me.

"Y-you're Naomi Marvel." I thought about denying what she was saying, but I decided not to. I nodded my agreement. "Holy shit. Oh sorry. What brings you into Plot Twists? And why are you looking at your own books?"

"Whenever I am traveling I like to go into the independent bookstores and look around, meet the shop owners, and yes, my ego gets the best of me, and I have to check to see if they carry my books in stock." We both chuckled for a moment. "I love the store, though. It feels very warm and inviting."

"That would be the owner's doing. I swear she would die if she knew you were in here. Can I get your autograph or something? I, I just don't think anyone is going to believe me that you were in here."

"Yeah, I'll sign an autograph for you. Is the owner in so that I may speak with her?"

"She's actually down in the archives vault. We had a request for a very rare book and she is checking to see if we have a copy."

"Really?" I asked. In my experience, it is rare for small bookstores to carry books that are supering rare, let alone to have a vault to store them in. I was becoming more and more impressed.

"Yeah, but if you are in town tomorrow, she will be working the store by herself from eight until noon. You'll have her as a captive audience."

"Thank you. I will stop in and introduce myself."

"Oh, I don't know if you'll need to introduce yourself, she's a huge fan of your books. Your last one she opened the box as soon as it arrived and didn't come out of her office until she had finished it."

"Wow, I'll definitely stop in then."

I signed the autograph for the woman and then went back to the hotel. It hadn't been a long day, but I was tired and just wanted relax.

As I lay on the bed with my computer next to me, I saw a message from Sydney pop up. It made me smile. It had only been a couple of days since we'd talked, but I missed her.

Sydney: Hey Stranger!

Naomi: Hey you! How are you?

Sydney: I'm good. How are you? Where've you

been?

Naomi: I'm good. I'm still out of town on business. Talk about a wasted trip. Everything these execs told me I had already found on the Internet.

Sydney: Out of town sounds fun. Did you get set up in a fancy hotel?

Naomi: Sort of. They have the hotel called Jungle. It is pretty neat. Each floor is themed after something dealing with the jungle. My floor is the rainforest.

Sydney: So, top floor for you? Just kidding.

Naomi: No. I'm sure I shouldn't complain, but I got room 1313. Do you think its bad luck?

Sydney: Nah, they cancel the bad luck out when you double them like that.

Naomi: Liar

Sydney: Maybe. Listen, I hate to cut this short, but I have to run out for a little bit. Are you going to be around online all night?

Naomi: Yes, I'm going to put on my jammies and chill in bed for the rest of the night.

Sydney: Great, hon. I'll catch you later then.

Naomi: I'm looking forward to it. ;)

Yes, I flirted with her. Sydney and I had stepped up our friendly flirting in the past couple of weeks. We were both involved with someone, but we were both missing something in our relationships.

After talking with Syd, I decided to flip channels and see what if anything I could find. I was surfing when I heard a knock at the door. I got up and checked my appearance in the mirror as I passed it. I was looking comfortable. When I opened the door, there she was, standing directly in front of me. How? Where did she come from? Oh god, she is beautiful. It was only a fraction of a second between my hearing the door close and when I found my back pressed against the wall. Her lips were moving with mine, my hands held above my head. I arched into her body seeking to feel more, to feel her closer. The room was filled with the sounds of our moans and gasps for breath.

Sydney moved her hands from above my head; her fingers trailing slowly down my extended arms. "Keep them up there," she said in a husky, lust filled voice.

"Oh god, yes," I responded.

As her lips frantically moved along my neck, I felt her hands circle my waist and slide down the back of the shorts I was wearing. She cupped my butt and pulled me tight against her. I couldn't help it and let out a low growl. There was a primal need growing between us. A need to consume the other.

"Are you sure?" she asked, pulling away from my neck. Her eyes were dilated, her breathing ragged.

"Yes," I whispered. I don't think I have ever wanted anything or anyone in my life more than I wanted her at that very moment.

Sydney leaned in slowly and our lips met again. This time there was more than lust, there was passion and love that could be felt through the kiss. I wrapped my arms around her neck, holding her lips to mine. Our tongues fought for dominance.

Slowly, never parting, we walked to the edge of the bed. Pulling back, our eyes meeting, the question hanging in the silence of the room broken only by the pounding of our hearts. With unspoken consent, I began undressing her. As I removed each piece, I marveled at the beauty standing before me. Her skin so soft, the paleness inviting. I was startled for a second as I felt her start removing my shirt. Once all our clothing had been removed, we made our way to the center of the bed. We lay there on our sides, our bodies just a hair's breadth apart.

"You...you take my breath away," I said, cupping her cheek with one hand. I leaned forward, pulling her lips to meet mine. The kiss started cautiously but was overtaken by the fire burning inside.

Sydney pushed me onto my back and covered my body with her own. The feel of her skin on mine was like fire, I needed more. Before I could think my hands were again positioned above my head.

"Do you know how long I have dreamed about this day? Imagined what your skin would feel like. Imagined how your body would respond to mine," said Sydney, her eyes tracing the length of my body.

"Stop imagining," I replied in my most seductive tone. I saw a wry smile cross her face. Her eyes locked with mine, and then as I watched she lowered her head and kissed each of my breasts softly, sucking on the nipple before releasing it. "Oh yes."

"Lay back and enjoy," Sydney whispered.

My breath caught at the tone in her whisper, the pure lust in her eyes overtook me. Slowly, methodically I felt her tongue gliding down my breast bone, over my stomach, as she made her way down to rest between my legs. I could feel her breath on my inner thighs. It had been a long time since I had felt something so intimate, damn it felt amazing.

Sydney's tongue began to move tentatively at first through my heated sex before I felt her take my clit into her mouth and begin to suck on it. She was slow and tender to start with, but then as we fell into a rhythm and need appeared to have taken over and she began to lap at my wetness and suck on my clit harder. I felt her enter me with two fingers. Long, slow, and deep strokes until I couldn't hold on any longer and I came, calling out her name.

Sydney made her way back up my body and I flipped our positions and showed her how amazing we were together. We came together several more times before she was overtaken by exhaustion.

I watched her sleep for a while before drifting off myself. I woke a few hours later, her strong arms wrapped around me. At first, I thought it was a dream until I felt her lips graze my neck. Maddie never did that. We'd been together for several years; she never once in that time kissed my neck liked that.

"Mmmm," I moaned. Damn this woman was good with her lips.

"Good morning," she whispered into my neck.

I turned to face her. "Good morning." I leaned in and kissed her, softly at first, but then the urge grew, as did the kiss. "Syd? How did you know? Where?"

"You were in my bookstore last night."

"Plot Twists?" Sydney nodded. "How did you know though?"

"I heard you talking with Natalie. I'd recognize your voice anywhere."

"Why didn't you say something then?"

"You were just leaving, and I knew that wasn't the place. So…"

"You messaged me to find out where I was," I finished for her as she smiled sheepishly at me. Her smile melted everything inside me. "God, you are more beautiful than you were in my imagination and dreams."

We came together in a slow and passionate kiss. Our bodies melted into one, and we were lost in each other again. We made love for hours. Well, now it's love, then, it was pure lust. After a short nap, we got dressed and ordered room service.

"I can't believe that you're here," I said, sitting down on the couch and feeling Sydney's arms wrap around me.

"There is no place that I would rather be." She kissed the side of my head and pulled me closer.

"What about--"

"We're separated, and she's out of town. It's just us right now. Let's enjoy our time together."

We sat there wrapped in one another's arms, enjoying the time together. We talked about the stuff we always talked about, books, writing, science, and life. It was such an amazing feeling. This is what I had been missing for so many years.

It wasn't long before Sydney told me that she had to get going. We said our goodbyes, we kissed for a long time, and then she was gone. I was leaving in the morning and really, I didn't want to.

Sydney and I spent the next six or seven months talking online, and when the opportunity presented itself, we spoke on the phone. Whatever it was we had was growing, and she was becoming a part of my life that I couldn't live without. I know Maddie could tell, we fought often about how I had changed, but Syd and I agreed not to tell anyone why or what had changed us.

It was after a particularly bad fight with Maddie that my life changed in ways I never would have thought possible. In both good and bad ways. This was also the source of my nightmares.

As I sat there, my heart pounding in my chest, my knuckles white from the grip I had on the steering wheel. I felt the impact of the car on the concrete barrier. I could hear the grinding of the metal as the speed and force sent the car careening down the roadway causing my head to hit the steering wheel. I could see, I think it was in the mirror, or maybe an out of body experience, but my blonde hair was being coated with blood from the cut I had sustained. I could smell the gas fumes around me, but I couldn't move. I'm not sure if it was fear or more than that, but I just sat there. And then it went black, no sights, no sounds, no scents, just black.

I remember waking with a start. The jolt to my body made the pain throughout burn like the flame of a torch. Searing and unforgiving. I could hear the machines beeping. I could smell the sterile air. That medical sterile, stale, recycled for your convenience air. As I opened my eyes, I was able to see the machines positioned around the bed, the IV pole with three bags of clear unassuming liquid hung on it. I followed the tube from the bottom of the bags to my left arm. There, I saw a board taped over the IV in my arm. I couldn't imagine what it would be for, or where I was other than in some hospital. I looked up and saw the blah beige walls decorated only with a clock, a whiteboard with Nurse Abby written on it, and a sad looking painting of some flowers in a vase. As I tried to look around the room, I turned my head and the room began to spin like a roulette wheel. I placed my bet at that moment that whatever was in me was coming out. I could feel the bile and acid traveling up my throat. I tried to will it down, but that didn't work. I tried to hold it down, yet that was even less successful and more painful.

"Here," said a woman's voice, and then there was a plastic puke tub in front of me. "Don't hold it in, just let it out."

I noticed the caring tone in the woman's voice and relaxed. I felt compelled to comply with this mysterious woman. As much as I hated the idea, I let go of the contents that were burning its way through my throat. When I was done, which felt like an eternity but for all I know was like ten seconds, the tub was moved and a cool wet rag was placed on the back of my neck as another one wiped the remaining toxic sludge from my mouth.

"You sustained a pretty serious head injury. Moving your head too quickly, well, that isn't recommended."

"Recommended by who?" I asked. "Where am I? How long have I been here?"

"Recommended by your body mostly. But the doctors and I strongly recommend listening to your body on this one. You're in the hospital. You've been here for four days." The woman moved so that I could finally see her without having to turn my head. "Do you remember the accident that brought you here?"

I, by instinct, moved my head slightly as if to shake it, but as the room started to spin I stopped and whispered, "No, I don't remember anything about an accident."

"Do you know your name?"

After several minutes of contemplation, strain, struggle, internal admonishing, I replied softly, "No, I don't know who I am, where I am, or even who you are."

"Well, it will come back to you. I'm Nurse Abby. I'm the day nurse. My name is written on the whiteboard over there." Abby pointed toward the whiteboard I had seen in my brief glance around the room.

My eyes moved to meet Abby's eyes. "Do you know my name?" After I asked I felt rather stupid. I mean, who has to ask others if they know who they are. I should know this information.

"I'm sorry, I guess that was pretty rude of me not to tell you what your name was. When you were brought into the ER the paramedics said the name on your driver's license was Naomi Marvel."

"Naomi...Marvel...that doesn't sound familiar at all. Would it? Should it? I mean, it's my name; it's who I am. Right?"

Abby must have seen the confusion building in my eyes. "It depends, honestly. For some people hearing their name causes a feeling of familiarity or comfort, for others, nada, nothing at all, I could be talking gibberish. You aren't the first person, and you won't be the last, who doesn't recognize or feel anything when they hear their name. What you need to do is not stress on it, because if you do, it isn't going to come to you. I know, I know, it is easier said than done, but please, trust me on this. I'm not supposed to tell you a lot about what happened, the doctors want to see what, if anything, you remember." Abby watched me for a minute and I could feel the fear welling up inside me. "Relax, please. You were in a car accident. And you were damn lucky to come out of it alive from what they have told me."

"W-was anyone else hurt?" I heard myself ask. Why couldn't I remember anything? What if I hurt or killed someone? Not that I want to remember that, but I mean...

"No, the police officer said that it was just you, well you and your car as it was wrestling with a guard rail. I'm not sure what the guardrail did to you first, but your car did a number on it. I've seen the pictures in the paper." We laughed for a minute, it felt good. I could feel my fears easing up slightly. "Well, your sense of humor is intact. I think that is a good sign that you are going to recover just fine."

Her tone seemed encouraging. "I, um, is there, well is anyone looking for me?"

"There was a woman that stopped by yesterday.

You weren't awake yet, obviously, so she said she'd come back again today, but I haven't seen her yet."

Just then, the door opened and a raven-haired woman entered wearing faded jeans and a brown leather bomber jacket. I saw her quickly scanned the room and then her eyes met mine.

"Hello, may I help you?" asked Abby.

"Hi, I'm um, Maddie. I'm a friend of Naomi's."

Maddie was a tall woman, she wasn't thin, but she couldn't be categorized as overweight either. She had raven black hair, crystal blue eyes, and a fair to almost pale complexion definitely caught your eye. All I could do was just stare at her with a blank look on my face. I didn't recognize this woman. I didn't get a vibe from her good or bad.

"I'm sorry, you are going to have to let me know how we know one another," I said, looking down at the tube going into my arm.

"What do you mean?" Maddie asked.

"Naomi has had," Abby started before looking to me. I nodded my approval for her to continue. "Naomi has had a pretty severe head injury and right now has amnesia. So, as her nurse, I need to remind you that Naomi has been through a lot, we are trying to keep her calm..."

"Why do you think I would upset her?" snapped Maddie.

"I didn't say that you would upset her, I said that we were trying to keep her calm. There is a difference." I could hear Abby's tone becoming cold and defensive. What was she picking up about this woman that I wasn't? "She has been through a lot, her body has sustained a lot of trauma."

"Yeah, the machines, tubes, and bandages give

that away."

"Um, I'm sitting right here. Can you not talk about me as if I'm not?" I had had enough of being ignored. I didn't know either of these women, but dammit I wasn't going to sit here and just be talked about. I had self-respect...right?

"Sorry. Here is the remote for the bed, the television, and the nurse call button. I'll be back in a bit to check on you and take your vitals." Abby handed me the corded white remote. "Don't push yourself. This is actually the longest that you have been awake and it is going to take its toll on you."

"I won't, I promise," I said as I watched her look at Maddie before exiting the room.

"So, how do we know one another?" I asked.

"Well, we were a couple for several years."

"And when did we break up?"

"The day of the accident. You stormed out of the house and then two hours later the police showed up at the house telling me you were in an accident."

"I see." So, what I had just learned was that I was a lesbian, I had been in a relationship, and just before my accident my girlfriend and I had broken up. I think that I understand why it is that I forgot this stuff. Maybe it wasn't just the head injury.

Just as I was about to start speaking a woman burst into the room. She looked frantic, scared, and gorgeous. I felt a connection to this woman and I don't know why.

"Naomi?" she asked.

"Who are you?" asked Maddie, her voice defensive.

"I-I'm Sydney. We're, um friends."

"How did you know she was here?"

"I called the hospital after not hearing from her for a few days. That isn't like her." Sydney made her way over to stand on the opposite side of the bed.

"Maddie, just go. If we broke up I'm no longer your responsibility," I said, sounding unsure of myself.

"I'm not leaving you with a complete stranger."

"Just go," I said with more force.

"Call me if you need anything," she said, writing her number on the pad of paper next to me. As she left, Maddie glanced back one last time.

"I'd ask how you are doing, but I talked to the nurse and she told me you had amnesia. Are you sure you are okay with my being here?" asked Sydney.

"Yes. I don't know how to explain it, but I feel a connection with you."

"That's good. Why don't I tell you about us?" Sydney sat on the edge of the bed and began telling me our story.

As Sydney spoke she cautiously moved closer, her hand eventually taking mine. The sheer honesty and love that shown in her eyes told me she was telling the truth. I'm not sure why, maybe it was the romance of the story, but I leaned forward and kissed her. It was a tentative kiss, but the surge of emotions it set off inside me caused me to begin to cry.

Abby entered while Sydney was trying to calm me down. I made sure that she knew that it was tears of happiness that were flowing. Sydney stayed there with me night and day until they were ready to release me. Maddie had told me where we lived and said that she would stay elsewhere while I was healing and we'd discuss things later. Sydney and I worked for the next month trying to recover my memories.

One day Sydney came up behind me and wrapped her arms around my waist and kissed the side of my head. It was then, that simple gesture that she had done several times since I was released from the hospital, that my memory came back, and that I realized how much I truly loved the woman holding me. Since that day, her arms have been my safe place. Nights like tonight, when I have nightmares about that car accident, Sydney pulls me into her arms and holds me close. It is then that I know she's got me.

BL Clark lives in Southern Wisconsin. As a child, she dreamed of becoming an author. She is now living her dream. In her free time, you can find her working on various story ideas, or playing with some form of technology.

Website: http://blc.bkclark.net

Happy Apples

Sallyanne Monti

October 2015 - Greenwich Village, NYC

*I*t wasn't until many years later that I could look *back and really see how scared I was of our connection. Back then all I could do was run."*

Kat told me this as we lay naked in each other's arms, intertwined in a desperate attempt to get as close as we possibly could.

"Back then I was petrified. I knew if you ran again, I couldn't stay anymore."

I told her this as I pressed my ear to her bare chest, to listen to her heart that belonged to me, as mine belonged to her.

We were determined not to repeat the mistakes of the past, mistakes that had cost us the last twenty-five years of our lives. We were in our early thirties then, seemingly ready to meet the love of our lives. When we did, it was catastrophic. I was determined to sweep her off her feet and Kat was scared to death. I believed that love would conquer all and Kat believed that it would suffocate her. Kat wanted time alone; I wanted only time with her. She ran, I begged, she came back, I held my breath. Then Kat didn't come back, and I had no breath left to give anyone.

This was the vicious cycle of our love. Hurtful, destructive and built on a foundation of fear and fabricated obstacles. We never said what we meant, we never meant what we said and everything went terribly wrong. But our love, oh our love, it was the to-die-for love, the love so great it hurts deep inside you all the time; the ever-constant lump in your throat and ache in the middle of your chest, that lets you know that you are alive, more alive than you've ever been in your life. Kat was perfect, perfect for me; perfect enough for me to wait twenty-five years for fate to bring us back together.

Despite the wasted decades and our joy at finally being together again, the pain of loss was still raw and the fear of abandonment floated just beneath the surface of our fragile rekindled love.

October 1990 - Park Slope Brooklyn:

We met at the supermarket, in the produce department of Key Foods, on a cold and windy October evening in Brooklyn in 1990. Our fingers brushed as we both grabbed for the last package of Happy Apples; those caramel enrobed Granny Smiths, stuck to their plastic shrink wrap, held upright only by the pointy wood stick handles, piercing their apple cores.

I had spent an extra thirty minutes exercising that morning, in anticipation of curling up in front of my fireplace, with a good book, a cozy blanket and this yummy pre Halloween treat.

I was officially cranky. My exhausting day of long meetings and client issues, and the commuter packed rush hour subway ride home had caught up with me. Granted it was only five stops on the F Train from my Carroll Gardens Bergen St. Law Office to my 9th Street & 7th Avenue Brownstone in Park Slope.

On an aggravating day like today, even after my

5:30 a.m. gym workout, I would have come home, run up to my fourth floor apartment, torn off my business suit and heels, pulled on my sweats and sneakers, grabbed my Sony Walkman and headed off for a run in Prospect Park, to blow off steam. On this particular night, the Happy Apples had won out over the run, and the anticipation of their sugary gooeyness had left me aching, in an eager sweet tooth sort of way.

It took all of my self-control, to not rip the plastic-covered apples out of my fellow shopper's hand. As I held on to my end of the wrapper, I looked down at the barren supermarket display, hoping that there was one more pair of these sticky treats hidden behind the caramel wraps, typically purchased by do-it-yourself candy apple makers. There wasn't.

As my gaze continued downward, I noticed her paint-splattered pink high-top sneakers. Who in their right mind would wear an expensive pair of Keds while painting? I thought. And who in their right mind would buy pink sneakers?

I was hoping my gentle tug on the Happy Apple packaging would release the sweet bounty into my palm. I was wrong. As I felt the distinct pull of resistance against my fingers increase, I thought to myself, if she doesn't let go of these damn apples, this could get ugly. Then I slowly looked up and stared into the darkest pair of fiercely determined eyes I'd ever seen in my thirty-two years. Immediately captured within the confines of her stern stare, I felt my heart rise up out of my chest and land smack dab in the middle of my stomach. Unbeknownst to me, this dive-bombing of emotions would become a pattern of infinite repetition in a love affair that would knock the living shit out of my insides and leave me aching for more than just a Happy Apple, on a regular basis and for decades to come.

On this, the day of our first fated encounter, I'd planned to give her my best legal argument for why these treats were mine and not hers. I almost said Possession is 9/10ths of the law as I continued to tug the coveted package in my direction. I stifled a giggle. As a corporate attorney, I clearly knew this saying wasn't a law at all.

Prepared to do battle, I felt the Brooklyn in me rise up from the bottom of my spine to the middle of my shoulder blades; the heat of annoyance surging like the mercury in a thermometer on a hot summer day. I felt the telltale signs of anger reach my green eyes as I took a deep breath, squared my shoulders, jutted out my ample chest and stared right back at her. As I opened my mouth to speak, I felt my voice catch in my throat as I said as firmly as I could, *"You don't really want to do this tonight do you?"*

I noticed that the soft pink color of her full lips almost matched the light pink of those ridiculous paint-splattered high-top sneakers. Her lips were heart shaped and had a soft shine from lip balm or maybe she had wet her lips before I'd lifted my head to stare into the face of the most adorable and intense woman I'd ever seen. She was playful yet extreme, she was soft and womanly yet unyielding and when she smiled her eyes came alive. Even then I thought adorable and intense, how can someone be a polar opposite of herself? I was affected. And my life would never be the same again.

She seemed equally affected. In the midst of our mutual fixed stare, she began to breathe faster and more deeply, I watched her small, round breasts rise and fall with the swell of her chest. Her light blue shirt was collarless, and clung to her flat stomach and tight abs, with the soft mounds of cleavage visible just below the

V of its neckline.

The thumb of her right hand was hooked through the front belt loop of her faded Levi's, her left knee bent as she calmly held on tightly to the Happy Apples with her other hand.

She was taller than my five-foot-four frame by about three inches. Her thick wavy hair was shoulder length and a soft brown, about two shades lighter than my own. Her dark brown almond-shaped eyes got even darker as her lips formed into a smirk. Her nose was straight and slightly rounded at the bottom, adding softness to her otherwise strict look. Her glasses sat atop her head as a makeshift hairband. She stared at me with shameless desire as her now lusty gaze moved down my body. I suddenly wished I'd changed into my sweats and running shoes. I felt exposed standing there in my fitted black business suit, pants hugging tightly to my muscular legs and thighs, jacket formed closely to my toned midriff and white silk shirt; as if she knew what I was thinking, her gaze stopped at the cleavage exposed by the top four open buttons of my shirt. In her brown eyes I saw arousal and a strange resolve for something I couldn't quite identify, at least not yet.

She would later tell me that, she saw anticipation and then kindness in my eyes. In that moment I felt like she saw through me, to the core of my being. In very short order I would give to her my heart, for what would inevitably be forever. In that moment, everything and everyone around us disappeared.

As I realized this woman could mean more to me than a quick sweet fix, I released my hold on the packaging and the Happy Apples fell into her tight grip. As they thumped against her left thigh, she smiled, a smile so magnificent that the dark recesses of her eyes twinkled to life, and in the radiance of her smile, my world stopped. How could I already love her, I didn't even know her? As she looked into the deep recesses of my soul, she saw the moment my heart attached itself to hers; and in her panic she thought to herself, *"I won't love her, I don't even want to know her."*

In less than five minutes, the tone of our relationship had been set. I would do everything in my power to love her and she would do everything in her power to not love me.

I pulled a business card out of my purse. As I handed it to her I said, *"I guess you win this one."* She pulled her own card out of the back pocket of snug jeans. As she handed it to me, she said, *"I always win."* Then she turned around and walked away, tossing the Happy Apples into her cart as she went. The card in my hand I read:

Kat Rands, Artist
Abstract Expressionism
Rands Gallery
217 Seeley St., Brooklyn, NY

Abstract Expressionism? And she always wins. This can't be good. As I hunted for my consolation indulgence, some dark chocolate and a bottle of Pinot Noir, I considered dumping her card into the supermarket trash bin. Instead I tucked it inside my purse.

The next day when I arrived at the office, there was a voicemail from her. *"Hi Abi Taylor, Attorney at Law. This is Kat Rands. I stole your Happy Apples last night. I mean you gave me your Happy Apples last night. I mean I won the Happy Apples fair and square last night. I mean I can't stop thinking about your white silk blouse and your brilliant green eyes. Will you have lunch with me? Call me at 718-222-0122, if you want to that is, which of course I know you do."*

Her voice was husky with the slightest of a N.Y. accent. I imagined her sitting in her gallery wearing her paint-splattered pink high-tops, while she leaned over a paint-stained drawing table, leaving me that message while she congratulated herself for being so witty and charming. Then I scolded myself for ignoring the warning signs of the inevitable havoc a free spirit artist such as she would undoubtedly wreak on my logical attorney disposition. We had nothing in common, I thought as I picked up the phone and dialed her number. She answered on the first ring and said *"Vito's Pizza, 9th & 7th, one p.m. today. Be there."* And she hung up.

What the fuck had just happened? She hung up on me. And for the second time in less than twenty-four hours, I was left dumbfounded in the wake of a whirlwind of a woman that would consume my every waking thought and lead me to do things so completely out of character that I would come to not even recognize myself. Even as I said the words out loud, *"She's got a long wait if she thinks I'm meeting her for lunch,"* I knew without a doubt, I would be meeting her for lunch today.

Pizza, the common ground to anything and everything; she can't be all bad if she chose pizza, my ultimate favorite food on the planet, for our first lunch together. Already I was thinking there would be more lunches. Things were moving too fast, too soon. I was too attached to an overly attractive woman, with a penchant for winning and wooing via shock appeal.

I wondered if she was a pizza purest like me, or a toppings-run-a-muck type of gal. She ordered hers with black olives and mushroom, with a Diet Pepsi. I ordered a cheese slice and a Diet Coke. She didn't take kindly to my comment that Diet Pepsi tasted like Raid Bug Killer. I ignored her attempts to incite a full on argument when she said Diet Coke was Devil Juice that rotted your brain and made grown women do crazy things. I said *"Oh like steal Happy Apples from unsuspecting attorneys in a supermarket?"* We both laughed.

I noticed how Kat's eyes crinkled in the corners when she laughed, and how her thick hair bounced below her ears as her head flew back in a hearty chuckle. As we sat across from each other with our pizza growing cold and our drinks getting warm, afternoon shoppers and young professionals paraded past our booth near the 7th avenue window of this popular pizza joint, on a bright and sunny fall day. *"So you're an artist,"* I said. *"All day, every day"* Kat answered. *"Well then, are you going to show me your etchings?"* I teased. *"Are you going to show me your legal briefs?"* she said without missing a beat. We looked at each other for a long time, each of us contemplating where this all might lead and how it might fit into our busy young lives. Life altering distractions are never convenient.

And I was distracted, very distracted. I could look into her eyes forever. They were an oddly dark brown, almost vacant, until she amused herself, which seemed to happen often. Then they were alive with laughter; Kat's thick lashes feathering the high cheekbones on her adorable yet striking face. I could see the golden highlights in her shoulder length hair, not visible the night before under the supermarket fluorescent lighting.

Kat told me she was an abstract artist. I would soon come to see how seriously she understated her talent.

On our second date, we met in her gallery, where she handed me a glass of Pinot Grigio Wine in a delicately engraved stemmed glass. The hummingbirds on the glassware didn't seem to mesh with the woman who had created the many dark canvases that filled the walls of the room. As she walked me through corridor after corridor of charcoal smeared images, the grey cloud-like objects seemed desolate and sad and then evolved to what could only be described as angry and furious. I soaked up every inch of each canvas, trying desperately to imbed them in my memory.

For a moment I remembered the spots of brightly colored paint on Kat's pink high-top sneakers, and wondered where the origin of this colorful splatter lived, as there was no evidence that I'd seen anywhere in her art or in the gallery. There was a story being told here of that I was certain, and in the erratic smudges of her charcoal drawings, it was profoundly sad. As we walked side-by-side, sipping wine I reached out and touched her hand. Kat swung around and faced me and pulled her hand away as if my touch had burned her skin. I reached for her wine glass and put both of ours down on a nearby bar height table that held her business cards and postcards of upcoming events.

I continued to hold her dark questioning gaze, afraid to take my eyes off her, intuitively knowing she would retreat into herself if I did.

I raised my hand to her cheek, involuntarily closed my eyes and inhaled deeply as the palm of my hand brushed the silkiness of her face. She was exquisitely a woman, and yet her hardness lingered beneath the surface. In that instant, I knew Kat was in severe pain and that her pain would steer the course of our new relationship. I was hopeful then, and believed that within the strength of my own hard-wired logic I could ease her unknown pain.

With my palm still lightly touching her cheek, I put my other hand around Kat's waist and pulled her towards me. As she began to pull away from me, I wrapped my fingers tightly around the soft cotton of her pink flannel shirt. I'd purposely let go of my grip in the supermarket and let her have her way with the Happy Apples. I wouldn't make the same mistake twice.

I lowered my hand from her cheek and wrapped my arms around her waist, putting my thumbs through her belt loops, gently squeezing her body to mine. I heard her suddenly inhale and felt her body stiffen. I could feel the twitch of the muscles in her strong thighs, as they pressed against my own. I pushed the center of my body into hers. Kat moaned. With my thumbs still hooked in her belt loops, I slipped my fingers into the back waistband of her jeans and caressed her. I buried my face in her shirt, taking in all her smells - soap, artist's charcoal and a faint smell of wine.

I ran my hands up her back to her strong shoulders and back down again to her waist. As I leaned back to look into Kat's eyes, I slipped my hands under her shirt and ran them up the front of her body, stopping at the warm naked firm mounds of her breasts. As I caressed her in a circular motion, under the palms of my hands, in the firmness of her nipples, was the evidence of her desire for me. Kat's dark vacant eyes were smoky with desire, my green eyes boring into the depths of her, refusing to break the connection, innately knowing if I did, she would escape from me into whatever abyss tormented her soul.

Kat pulled me into another dark room. I felt an immediate and almost panicked urge to commit every detail of her to memory as if she would disappear from my life unexpectedly. In that moment, an overwhelming sadness came over me, as the undeniable thud of my gut told me our time together would be short lived. I pushed away this feeling of impending doom and allowed myself to be led to what felt like a futon, somewhere in the obscure landscape of the room. We held hands as she lowered me to the cushion. My eyes adjusted to the lighting in the room and Kat appeared naked in front of me, her small firm breasts erect with arousal and her soft mound of hair glistening in the moonlight streaming through the loft window. I quickly removed my clothes as she lowered herself on top of me and kissed me. Kat's lips were soft and warm and slightly wet. Our first kiss was tentative. As our kiss intensified and our tongues caressed, I lost myself in her mouth as I thought I could kiss her forever.

I slipped my hand between our bodies caressing her clitoris as she began to move on top of me. She arched back and I took her nipple into my mouth, circling it with my tongue and gently sucking, one breast at a time. She became more excited. I slipped my fingers inside of her. She began to moan and grind into me as my fingers beat within her, the rhythm of my newfound love. I was as aroused and as ready as she was. As Kat's hips moved feverishly, mine met hers with each thrust and grind. We were lost in each other and moaning, and as she kissed me harder and pushed her tongue deeper into my mouth, I surrounded it with what felt like the very core of my soul, as we came together in an arch of bodies and sweat and unexpected tears, professing our love for each other in the dark of her gallery.

The next day when I arrived at my office, I saw the blinking light of a phone message. I was giddy with excitement as I was sure it was Kat who had left me the voicemail. As I sat at my desk, I leaned back in my chair and pushed the listen button. My heart rose up and jumped out of my chest at the sound of her voice. By the end of the voicemail it had effectively landed in the pit of my stomach. I was crushed. *"I'm sorry Abi, but I can't do this. Its not you, it's me. I shouldn't have led you to believe I was available, because I'm not. I'm sorry. Please don't call me."* I leaned over my desk, put my head in my hands and wept.

Kat would come back to me after this and leave me many times over the next year, too many times to count. In a moment of accidental vulnerability, as she would come to call it, Kat explained that the only person she had ever trusted with her heart had left her in the throes of passion to return to her suburban life and her suburban wife, in a residential neighborhood in Queens.

I loved Kat unconditionally, her heart, her soul, her humor, her body and her talent. She was perfect. We were perfect together. Each time Kat returned I gave her more and more of my mind, my body, my love and every ounce of myself, believing that in doing so, she would surely know how completely I loved her and how I would never leave her. I had no shame, I cried, I sobbed, I begged Kat not to leave me, not to leave us and to please not run. *"I will love you forever, Kat. I can erase all your demons. Our love can conquer all. Please don't leave me. Trust me, trust you and trust fate."*

Each time Kat came back, she told me she loved me. She said I was her destiny and that she'd never let me go ever again. Our lovemaking was more and more intense and our resolve to stay together fierce. As our hearts grew closer; and in the moments when the intensity joined us as one, Kat would run. Each time she left me was worse than the time before.

She didn't want to be in a relationship, she needed her creative freedom, she was too young to be tied down and more often than not, our relationship simply didn't feel good to her, I didn't feel good to her. With each rejection, I fell further into the depths of despair, resolved to walk away from her when she came back, because eventually Kat would come back.

Her art was incredulous during these times, tortured and black with larger than life blurred images of women's bodies swirled through murky clouds and obscure impressions of a dark sun, desperate to break through the torrential rain. Nowhere in the soul of this woman I loved, was the evidence of the colorful joy that lived on the paint-splattered soles of her pink high-top sneakers.

Our love would follow the peaks and valleys of a dangerous snow covered mountain range, where the bright glare of the sun reflecting off the beautiful white hills drew you in and masqueraded as warmth that could satisfy your soul forever. In reality the frigid icy depths of despair were always on the verge of collapsing in a deadly avalanche.

After a passionate night of lovemaking, I fell peacefully asleep in Kat's arms as she spoke of watercolors of joy and speckled hues of brightness. Finally, Kat is mine and her darkness is vanquished.

When I woke up that morning she was gone and in her wake was a note.

Abi:
I can't handle the inevitable pain of losing you. Our relationship breaks my heart. It's not good for me. You're not good for me. I love you more than you'll ever

know, and this is why I must go.
    Kat

I spent the next twenty-five years of my life in heartbroken agony, knowing if Kat did return, it would be my turn to run. I was broken. I threw myself into health and fitness, a successful law career and building wealth. It was a lonely empty life, but it was my life. I dated other women from time to time. They were nice enough, the sex was nice enough, but none of them were Kat. She was my heart, she was my soul, she was my one and only.

Kat spent her twenty-five years, evolving into a renowned Artist, whose dark and dreary abstract canvases graced the walls of the rich and famous.

October 2015 - Carroll Gardens Brooklyn:

It was a chilly fall day in October 2015, when I returned from an arduous business trip. I was tired and not in the mood to go through the giant stack of mail on my desk.

About to call it a day, I noticed a handwritten envelope, in a familiar scrawl, a scrawl I'd know anywhere and one I hadn't seen in twenty-five years. I received the handwritten invitation from Kat to attend the opening of her new gallery on Christopher St. in Greenwich Village. In that moment, I relived the countless times my heart had soared in the hope Kat would chose me and our love only to end in the crushing throws of heartache. I was about to tear up the invitation and throw it into the recycling bin, when the undeniable thud of a gut feeling warned against it. I asked my assistant to hold my calls, kicked off my shoes, poured myself a glass of Pinot

Noir from the wine cooler in my office and sat down on the sofa across from my desk. My hands trembled as I tore open the envelope. As I pulled out the postcard, I expected to see the familiar dark and desperate shades of gray and black abstract art that was her signature, adorn the promotional card.

I heard an involuntary sob escape from my lips as I dropped my wine glass to the floor. I stared at the card trying to come to terms with the message. The images on the card were smudged in bright watercolor swirls. It announced:

An Exhibit by Kat Rands
Color My World
A Tribute to Abi
My One and Only

In Sharpie marker, on the back of the postcard, she had written.

Abi,
My One and Only Love,
I still love you with all my heart.
If you stay, I promise to never run again.
Kat

Again I felt my heart rise up out of my chest and land smack dab in the middle of my stomach. This dive-bombing of emotions as a result of deeply loving Kat for so long still left me aching for more. I put my head in my hands and sobbed, as I had two and half decades earlier.

I had every reason not to go, and a million more reasons not to trust her. We'd thrown away twenty-five years of our lives. When I walked into the gallery, I saw her standing wearing a pink flannel shirt, Calvin Klein jeans and the same pair of paint-splattered pink high-top Keds. She was thinner, her cheekbones sharper than I'd remembered. Her hair was streaked with white, her stylish rectangular dark frame glasses once used as a make-shift hairband, were now firmly planted on the bridge of her nose and her eyes were twinkling in the bright gallery lights. She never looked more beautiful. As Kat looked into my eyes she placed her right hand over her heart and closed her eyes, giving herself an imaginary hug.

I was much leaner and fit than she remembered. Later as we lay naked in bed, Kat told me I was toned and sexy, even sexier because I didn't have a clue as to how hot I really was. Although I liked hearing that she thought this, I found it silly and amusing. All I really wanted to hear was how she had never stopped loving me, how every day of the last twenty-five years she thought about me, and us. Kat told me how it had taken her this long to heal enough to come back to me whole and ready for the greatest love of her life.

As I felt the familiar stirrings of losing myself to this woman, I reached for her. As I drew Kat towards me, she began to pull away. Then she backed out of bed and out of the room. As I watched her naked body retreat into the darkness, I began to panic and cry. She reappeared and turned on the bedside table light.

As the tears streamed down my face, Kat looked down at me with her eyes twinkling. With a giant smile she pulled something out from behind her back and said: "*These are for you my darling love. We win.*" Cradled in the palm of her hands was a perfectly sealed package of Happy Apples.

Sallyanne Monti wrote her first compelling literary piece at age 5, with a red Crayola crayon; a profound note to her parents, returning allowance to help pay the bills.

It was the beginning of her love affair with storytelling and heartfelt confabulations of her exuberantly aware and overactive mind.

Afraid to Fall
Clarissa Thomas

Did you know that it only takes a moment to fall in love? I never believed it was possible, until I met her. My breath had caught in my lungs as I stared at her standing across the street from me, silently observing the argument that seemed to be breaking out in front of us. She didn't notice me, at least not at first, and I couldn't help drinking in the sight of her while the two men that had collided on the street while out for a jog distracted her. With beautiful chestnut hair pulled back into a long ponytail and eyes of sapphire, she was like a goddess.

My heart seemed to stop beating, just for a moment, when those beautiful blue eyes lifted to lock with my own emerald ones. I could see the confusion on her face as I stared at her in silence, not looking away from the beauty that seemed to hold me prisoner. But as they always do, the moment had to end.

I was released from her hypnotic gaze when a small blonde reached out and touched her shoulder, drawing my goddess's attention from me. I released a sigh of frustration, feeling an emptiness settle inside me as I watched the girl and the blonde walk away, leaving me standing there alone and wishing I knew something about her.

No matter how hard I tried, I couldn't seem to get her out of my head. Her beautiful blue eyes haunted my dreams, causing me to wake with a small smile on my lips every morning since the day I first saw her. She seemed to be everywhere, walking down the street in the opposite direction, driving the car sitting next to me at the stoplight. I had even seen her walk past me in the mall when I was in a rush to get to work. Each time I saw her, I tried to find some way to talk to her, some way to start a conversation, but nothing seemed to come to mind. My legs didn't want to listen to my brain, refusing to start walking in the direction she had been going. Instead, I just stood there watching her walk off, wishing I could approach her, over and over again.

Shaking the thoughts of her from my mind, I tried to focus the task I was currently working on. I had two days to get Old and Musty Books, the small bookstore where I was currently employed, decorated for Valentine's Day. My boss had given me a giant box of hearts and Cupids to put throughout the store any way I saw fit. Right now, I was on a ladder, hanging up a cluster of hearts around a baby Cupid when I heard the front door open behind me.

"I'll be with you in a second," I called out, not looking back at the customer that had walked in.

"Take your time," a woman's voice replied, so softly I almost didn't hear her.

I quickly finished hanging the red and pink hearts in that section of the store before climbing down the ladder and folding it to lay it against the wall. I forced a realistic smile to my lips and turned to face the customer that had entered while I was busy. Not seeing her in the main part of the store anymore, I shrugged and walked over to the counter, knowing if she needed any help, she'd come and find me at the front.

While waiting for the customer, I grabbed my

book from below the counter and started reading it. My boss didn't mind us reading as long as it didn't affect productivity. If a customer needed help or there was something that needed to be done, we were expected to handle those issues first. As I was reading, I heard footsteps approach the counter and looked up from my book, smiling at the sight of the small bundle of energy standing before me and rocking back and forth on her heals with a huge smile on her face.

"Hi, Kara," I said, smiling brightly at the hyper woman.

"Jess, you will never believe what just happened to me! I was walking down the street and this dog ran out in the middle of the road. I was so scared the poor thing was going to get hit, but the car that was driving by barely missed it. The dogs okay, but I'm pretty sure I suffered a major heart attack. I'm okay now though," Kara told me, smiling the whole time she was telling me her story.

"I'm glad both you and the dog are okay, Kara," I said, holding back laughter at her words.

"Me too," Kara said, running a hand through her long blonde hair before hopping up onto the counter and sitting down. "Did I tell you that I have a date this weekend?"

"Yes, you told me that when you came in here yesterday," I said, my green eyes twinkling in amusement as I watched the small blonde.

"Sorry, I'm just so excited. She's beautiful, and smart, and funny, and…"

"And sweet, and amazing, and perfect," I said, laughing at her obvious crush on this mystery woman. "Do I get to meet her?"

"Nope," Kara announced, giving me an evil smile

as her brown eyes sparkled with mischief. "You're too mean to meet her."

I gave her a mock look of pain, clutching my heart for dramatic effect. "You wound me with your words, my friend," I told her, holding back laughter as she rolled her eyes.

"Oh please. We both know nothing wounds you," Kara joked, shaking her head at me.

I started to respond to her when I heard a soft voice interrupt our fake argument. "Um, excuse me. Sorry to interrupt, but I was wondering if you can help me?" the voice from earlier said, drawing my attention away from Kara to assist the customer.

All thoughts and words disappeared as I stared into the familiar blue eyes from before. I couldn't seem to form any sentences to respond to the beautiful woman. Hell, I couldn't form any words as I was held captive by those beautiful eyes again.

"Jess?" Kara said, grabbing my shoulders and shaking me until I turned to look at her.

"Huh?" I mumbled, frowning at my friend in confusion.

"She said she needs your help with something, not your drool," Kara told me, giving me a look of disappointment.

"Sorry," I replied, wiping at my chin for any drool that might actually be there, grateful that I didn't feel any watery substance. I turned back to the brunette, careful not to look her directly in the eyes again. "How can I help you?"

"I was wondering if you had a certain genre of books? I've checked multiple bookstores around the area and none of them seem to carry it," my mystery woman told me.

"Most likely we do. What's the genre?" I asked, turning to my computer to search the database for whatever she was looking for.

"Oh, um, lesbian romance actually," she said, causing me to look back at her as she blushed in embarrassment.

"Oh, they definitely have that," Kara mumbled, earning a glare from me and a confused look from the brunette.

"Yeah, it's back here," I said, walking from behind the counter to show the girl where the books were. As I walked past Kara, I gave her a small push, nearly knocking her from the counter.

"Asshole!" Kara called out as I lead the beautiful woman to the books at the back of the store.

"Here you go. Lesbian romance," I said, pointing at the books in front of us.

"Thank you, Jess," the woman said, giving me a small smile.

I looked at her and frowned. "How do you know my name?" I asked, confused.

"Your friend said it earlier," the woman explained, causing me to blush when I remembered exactly why Kara had said my name in front of this beautiful stranger.

I nodded. "Yeah, right. She did," I mumble, embarrassed.

"Thank you again, Jess," she said.

"Yeah, no problem, Ma'am," I replied, turning to walk away when I felt a hand touch my arm. I glanced back at her in confusion and watched her remove her hand from my arm before holding it out to me.

"Shay Hunters," the beauty said.

I smiled brightly as I took Shay's hand in my own, giving it a firm shake. "Jessica Lawson, but everyone calls me Jess," I announced.

"It's a pleasure to finally meet you, Jessica," Shay said softly, giving me a mysterious smile.

"You can call me Jess. Everyone else does," I tell her, smiling at her as I stared into her beautiful blue eyes.

"Is it okay if I call you Jessica? I'd prefer not to call you what everyone else calls you," Shay admitted, blushing slightly at her own admission.

I smile at her words and nod. "I'd love that," I said, before noting I was still holding her hand.

After that day, Shay seemed to come into the store every day. She rarely bought anything, and spent most of the time talking to me about life and her fear of love. I learned that she was an accountant, and though she was good at what she did, she hated her job with every fiber of her being. She admitted that she believed true love was a myth, a story told to give people hope, when in reality, it was nothing but a cruel lie.

I confided in her about some of my past relationships, and about how cruel my former partners were. I told her about my parent's divorce, and my awful stepmother. I was amazed by how easily I could talk to her about everything, and how willing she was to listen to me rant.

One day when I was getting off work, Shay walked in and gave me a huge smile as she walked up to the counter to see me closing down the register. "Off work?" she asked.

"Almost. My replacement is in the back getting changed. I just have to close out the register and then wait for her to sign in."

"Awesome! So does that mean you have time to go get some coffee with me?" Shay wondered, giving me a small smile.

"Of course! Give me about five minutes and I should be ready to go," I promised, hurrying as I closed out the register.

I waited impatiently as Susan, my replacement, took her time to sign into her account on the register causing me to have to wait even longer to spend time with Shay.

"Do you need anything else?" I asked Susan, praying for once she would just let me leave.

"Um, no, I think I'm good this time. Enjoy the rest of your day," Susan said.

I gave her a small smile and waved, before joining Shay at the front of the store where she was currently sitting in one of the chairs used for reading. "Hey, you ready?" she asked, when I came to a stop in front of her.

"Yeah, let's go," I said, holding out my hand to help her to her feet.

Shay gave me a grateful smile after she got to her feet, before turning to walk out of the store, leading me through the mall towards one of the many coffee shops scattered throughout the shopping center. We each quickly ordered our coffees and took one of the small tables at the back of the little café.

"How has your day been?" I asked her, as I took a cautious sip of my coffee.

"I worked all morning," she said, shrugging and causing me to laugh.

"Why don't you like your job?" I asked, giving her a curious look.

"I just find it boring," she told me.

"Oh, okay," I said, watching her for a few moments before speaking again. "I still can't believe you're an accountant."

"Why is that so hard to believe?" she wondered, tilting her head slightly and giving me an amused look.

"It's not that it's hard to believe. I just didn't expect you to be an accountant. I figured you for the type to do something related to books because of how often you're in the bookstore," I explained, hoping I didn't insult her.

"Well, you see…I…um…I have a confession to make," she told me, giving me a sheepish smile.

"Okay," I mumbled, giving her a cautious look.

"I actually don't really read that much. I went to the bookstore to get a book for my friend as a joke," she explained, still looking nervous.

"Oh…"

"She's been picking on me lately and trying to make me blush by asking me random questions. It was embarrassing, and I got tired of answering her questions about lesbian sex and stuff, and figured I'd get her a book as a prank."

"So, are you a lesbian?" I wondered, making sure I wasn't hearing things.

"Huh?" she asked, before giving me a confused look. "Yeah, why?"

"No reason," I said, smiling brightly at her. "Can I ask you something?"

"You just did," she joked, her blue eyes shining brightly in amusement. "What do you want to ask?"

I rolled my eyes and tucked a strand of auburn hair behind my ear. "If you don't like to read, why did you keep coming into the Old and Musty?"

"Because they have this gorgeous cashier that I've been crushing on for months ever since I saw her standing across the street from me," she admitted, giving me an adorably flirtatious smile.

I returned the smile, feeling my heart beat speed up as we stared at one another for a long time in silence before I broke it. "Are you ready to leave?"

"Um, yeah," she said, frowning at me in confusion.

We walked from the café and out of the mall in silence. I watched as she started to head towards her car, only to grab her hand to stop her. "Do you want to go to the park? It's late enough that it won't be crowded, and I'd really like to spend some time alone with you."

I watched as a huge smile blossomed across Shay's face before she nodded and followed me to the park, still holding each other's hands as we walked in comfortable silence. We came to a stop in front of a large tree and sat down in front of it with our back's resting against its huge trunk.

As the silence drew out between us, I turned to look at her, feeling the need to stare at her overtake me. She must have felt me looking at her because not long after I had turned to admire her, her head moved to face me and our eyes locked once more. I smiled at her softly and watched a matching one grace her beautiful lips.

I don't know what came over me in that moment, but it was almost like someone else had control of my body as I leaned down and pressed my lips so softly against her own, feeling as though our lips belonged together. The shock that went through my body as her lips touched mine proved to me that this was right. Our lips were meant to be pressed together. I moaned into the kiss as a soft tongue pressed against my lips lightly, requesting entrance into my mouth. I opened my lips, allowing her tongue to explore without hesitation.

We stayed like that for a long time, lips moving together and tongues fighting for dominance until the sound of a cell phone ringing drew us out of the haze that was surrounding us.

Grumbling, I reached into my pocket and pulled out my phone, sparing a quick glance at the caller id. "What is it, Kara?" I ask, frowning.

"The date was amazing! She's incredible, Jess. Absolutely incredible! And she knows how to kiss a girl speechless. I swear I couldn't remember how to form words for a few minutes," Kara gushed, causing me to roll my eyes, and Shay to laugh lightly as she listened to the words.

"Kara, my friend. I love you and everything, but can I call you tomorrow so you can talk about your date? I'm kinda in the middle of something."

"Are you on a date? Why didn't you tell me you had a date, Jess? I thought I was your best friend?"

"Yes, I am on a date. I didn't tell you because I wasn't planning on going on a date until about ten minutes ago, and you are my best friend. Now can I please call you tomorrow?"

"Oh, of course! Then we can both talk about how our dates went! Love you, sweetie. Call me tomorrow," Kara said, before hanging up.

I sighed and hung up my own phone, giving Shay a sheepish smile. "Sorry about that. Kara is always a bit overenthusiastic."

"Don't worry about it. It's kind of endearing, actually. Besides, I have met her before, remember? The first time you and I talked she was there with you," Shay reminded me, giving me an amused look.

"Yeah, I forgot that you met her," I admitted, smiling at her.

Shay smiled back at me before her smile faded and a distant look entered her eyes. "What's wrong?" I asked, frowning at her.

"Can I ask you something?" she wondered, giving me a worried look.

"You just did," I replied, using her words from earlier. I smiled as a soft chuckle escaped her, and she rolled her eyes. "You can ask me anything," I promised.

"Do you believe in love at first sight?" she wondered, a cautious look on her face.

"Yeah, I do," I admitted, shrugging. "Why?"

"Because part of me wonders if I fell in love with you when I first saw you, or if it was just lust," she explained, worry clear in her eyes as she stared at me.

"What do you think it is?" I asked.

"I don't know."

"Do you want to figure it out?"

"How?" she asked, giving me a confused look.

"If it's lust, we can help you get past it now," I told her, watching her face as realization dawned on her.

"And if it's not?"

"Then we'll figure things out together," I promised, standing out and holding my hand out to help her up. "So how do you want to do this?"

She sighed, giving me a questioning look as if she was trying to see what I wanted, what I was feeling. I just gave her an encouraging smile, waiting for her to decide what she wanted. Finally, she gave me a small smile in return.

"I don't think I need to figure it out. I think I know the answer, but I'm too afraid to admit it," she told me, giving me a nervous smile.

"You can tell me," I whispered, reaching out to touch her cheek softly.

I felt my heart melt as she leaned into my touch, those beautiful eyes closing in contentment for a moment before opening to look at me once more. "I think I fell in love with you the moment I first saw you," she admitted, turning her head slightly to place a kiss on my palm.

"Same here," I said, smiling at her. "You captivated me and stole my heart."

Staring into each other's eyes, we leaned forward and brought our lips together in a soul-searching kiss. At that moment, everything in my life seemed to fall into place, and I knew without a doubt that this is where I belonged. Right here with her. I knew with all my soul that I had fallen in love with this beautiful woman, the goddess from across the street. My heart and soul belongs to Shay Hunter.

Clarissa Thomas is a young woman who lives alone with just the stories in her mind. She continuously travels with her job, never in the same place for longer than three years. With stories constantly fighting for the upper hand inside of her mind, Clarissa writes the worlds she imagines.

For Certain

Lucy J. Madison

Once or twice on the ride upstate, Casey's hand dropped down to the gear shift, on the off chance it grazed her leg. It was perfect late April afternoon with the weather unseasonably warm in the 70s. The drive would be a pleasant two hours from New York City to the Catskills in Casey's beloved black Jeep Wrangler with the soft top down.

Casey and Jess drove in silence for much of the time, both listening a bit too intently to the streaming indie rock playlist from Apple music. Casey was so close to Jess that it physically hurt her. It took every ounce of Casey's willpower not to reach out and touch her as they drove.

After a quick trip to the local grocery store to buy wine and food (in that order), they made their way down some winding back country roads to a cabin set on 11 acres of wilderness with no telephone, no television, and no Internet access. It was the perfect place to forget the world and figure out if Jess felt at all the way Casey did.

"I'm going for a walk, I need to stretch my legs." Jess said to Casey as she unpacked groceries. This was certainly not the way Casey wanted to set the tone for the next few days, but she sensed Jess needed a bit of space.

"Sure," Casey said. "See you later."

While Jess was gone, Casey took the opportunity

to familiarize herself with the cabin that her head coach owned as a vacation property and offered to Casey to get away. It was cozy, with wide planked hardwood floors and pine paneling. The kitchen was modestly stocked, with plenty of dishes, pots and pans. The dining table for two overlooked the backyard and the expanse of woods.

To the left of the kitchen was a small den with comfy chairs, a small couch and a large stone fireplace. The bedroom was to the right of the kitchen and was the largest room in the cabin, with a queen size bed and large paned windows providing a breathtaking view of the mountains. Casey unpacked her clothes in the dresser and placed Jess's bag on the pillow top bed with the hand-hewn log headboard, making it clear she expected her to sleep in bed and not on the couch, just in case there was any doubt. Just the thought of being in bed with Jess sent shivers down Casey's spine.

The spa-like bathroom took up the remaining back section of the cabin. In it was a large shower for two with a faux waterfall and about 20 different jets. Blurred glass provided light to the shower room, but also provided a fuzzy view of the shower from the kitchen, oddly enough. Casey made a mental note of that as she put her toiletries away.

With nothing else to do, Casey decided to sit down in the den and read, although she stared at the same page for about 10 minutes. She was not the type of person who brought random women to rustic cabins in the middle of nowhere. She was the type of person who thought a great deal but often didn't say much. After her last failed relationship of three years, Casey was nearly at the point of swearing off women, and relationships, all together. She was used to being alone and was okay with that. She had a good, happy life with her family and friends. But there was something about Jess. Something magical that she couldn't resist.

Casey heard the cabin door squeak open and pretended to be engrossed in her book.

"You need to come out with me. I found this really incredible place! C'mon, Casey."

"Okay! I'm coming," said Casey laughing at Jess's excitement.

Jess led Casey on a short walk down a path in the woods. Like a mirage, Jess found a cool and clear running stream with a deep pool.

"Isn't it beautiful?" Asked Jess, smiling broadly as she splashed Casey playfully. "It's like this secret place just for us."

The thought occurred to Casey that they could have been the only two people on the planet just then, laughing and splashing. They took turns sitting on a small rock so that the ice cold water could pour over their heads. Casey went first, then Jess. When Jess stood, she turned toward Casey. Her tee shirt clung to her body and water ran down her face. She looked at Casey and for a long moment, Casey could think of nothing else except kissing her. Jess was so alive, so amazingly beautiful, Casey couldn't tear her eyes away. Jess had to see it. She had to know how Casey felt. Casey could see Jess shivering. The water was almost icy and the outside temperature was cooling off fast.

"Let's go back to the cabin to warm up before we both get hypothermia," Casey suggested. They both hurried back to the cabin, shivering as the sun set over the mountains.

"I really need to take a hot shower," Jess announced the moment they walked in the door. "Put some music on, I'll be out in a few."

"Sure," Casey replied. "When you get out, we'll have dinner."

"Thank God! I'm starving."

Jess disappeared into the bedroom and came out a minute later. "Where the hell is the shower in this place?"

Laughing, Casey showed her the shower room.

"Wow! This is amazing," Jess said as Casey turned on the 20-jet shower. Casey was fully aware that she was blushing hard and was as turned on as the shower was. She muttered something about the music and extricated herself as carefully as she could from the bathroom before she lost every ounce of self control she possessed.

Casey tried to keep busy. She dried off as best she could and changed into a pair of sweats and a sweatshirt. She set up her Bluetooth speaker and settled on The Clientele. Since it was now a little chilly in the cabin, she lit a fire in the fireplace and began to make dinner. While she sautéed some chicken and vegetables, Jess showered. Every five seconds or so, Casey peeked from the kitchen to the leaded glass of the shower. Although she couldn't see Jess clearly, she could just make out the outline of her dancer's five-foot-six body, her long blond hair flowing down to the middle of her back. Tearing her eyes away was a chore for Casey. Keeping herself from entering the shower with her was difficult. Trying not to burn dinner to a crisp was nearly impossible.

⚜⚜⚜

The first moment Casey saw Jess, she felt this immediate recognition, like they had known each other forever and she was just seeing her after a long time apart. Casey had just finished her first season as an assistant basketball coach for Fordham University's women's basketball program and was settling back into a regular routine as spring began to thaw the frozen New York ground.

One morning after her workout, Casey bumped into Jess as she was leaving a dance studio. Casey muttered something unintelligible as she stared into Jess's crystal blue eyes that were so clear, so wide open and trusting, Casey was locked in and couldn't even blink. Casey excused herself, smiling broadly at Jess, and Casey felt as if she had been hit head on by a Mack truck.

For the next few weeks, they saw each other more and more often in and around the athletic center (mostly because Casey carefully noted Jess's schedule). Casey checked around and found out Jess was an accomplished modern dancer and a new faculty member in the B.F.A. Program in Dance co-run with the Alvin Ailey Dance Company. Apparently Jess specialized in Taylor-based modern dance although Casey had absolutely no idea what that actually meant. Ask her about a motion offense or a two-three zone defense and she could talk for 15 minutes. Ask her about modern dance and she became an instant idiot.

Their chats before and after workouts grew longer and longer, so one day Casey took a flying leap and invited Jess out for lunch. She felt like lunch was safe. It wasn't really a dinner date, but it was something a little more serious than grabbing a cup of coffee. All of this spontaneous flirting was wildly unlike Casey since she really was an analytical type of person who measured everything and never dove headlong into anything except a pool on a hot summer day. Casey's trusty Gay-dar was telling her that Jess was gay, but how many lesbian female modern dancers does anyone really know? To her surprise, Jess accepted.

That lunch lasted over two hours. Casey learned that they had much more in common than she originally thought. Both of them grew up in small towns, both of them had one other sibling – an older brother – and both were obsessed with something. In Casey's case, it was basketball. In Jess's, dance. Both knew what it was like to sacrifice and train to be the best they could be. For Casey, it was so comforting to be around someone who totally got her point of view and passion for basketball.

Casey's head was spinning. The air between them tingled with electric energy and somehow made Casey feel more like herself than she ever had around another person. Jess had an easy-going manner and her laugh was infectious. Casey stared at Jess's lips and wondered what it would feel like to kiss her. She was simultaneously awestruck and completely content and it unnerved her.

"Casey, I bet you'd get along great with my girlfriend," said Jess nonchalantly as she re-wrapped a light blue scarf around her neck that matched her eyes.

And there it was. The hammer had just been dropped. The good news was that apparently Casey's Gay-dar was working just fine, but the bad news was that her Single-and-Available meter was definitely in need of servicing. Come to think of it, that wasn't the only thing in need of servicing.

Casey made some excuse about a scouting trip to Pennsylvania and excused herself within minutes after the girlfriend comment. Jess seemed utterly confused by Casey's sudden shift but Casey really didn't care. She had to get out of there fast. On her walk back to her apartment, Casey mentally listed the litany of reasons why this instant attraction to Jess should be, must be, ignored. First, this job as assistant basketball coach of a Division I program was a big step in her career and she needed to stay focused in the off-season. Second, Jess had a girlfriend. And third, Jess was a dancer for Christsakes. Despite all the rational reasons Casey could come up with to block any romantic feelings from her mind, Jess's beep blue eyes and penetrating stare weren't too easily removed from Casey's thoughts or fantasies.

Three weeks later, Casey continued to ignore Jess's pleading texts to meet up and talk. She purposely went to the athletic center during off hours when she was sure not to run into Jess. Casey knew she was being childish. She knew Jess would just want to be friends but that just wasn't at all what Casey wanted. In the short time Casey had known Jess, she knew that anything less than having all of Jess was a waste of time. She didn't know much, but at least she was self-aware enough to know that.

One evening, Casey worked out alone in the empty gym – just her and a basketball. Basketball had always been her savior, and any chance she could get to lace up her sneakers and shoot a basketball was a welcome relief from the endless thoughts rattling around in her head. Casey was so lost in her own thoughts she didn't even hear the gym doors click closed. Her jump shot fell short and the ball bounced off the rim and headed toward center court. Casey ran to track it down. She picked up her head and saw Jess holding the ball, standing at center court.

"You've been avoiding me," Jess said quietly, handing the ball back to Casey.

"Maybe a little," Casey replied honestly.

"Why?"

"Because you have a girlfriend." Casey wiped

the sweat from her face with the front of her tee shirt, showing off her hard stomach. Jess stared at her stomach and blushed.

"We're not serious" was all Jess could manage.

Casey wasn't sure what to do next. Every muscle in her body was arching toward Jess. Before she could stop herself, Casey's hand was on Jess's face, her thumb tracing Jess's jawline.

"Come away with me," Casey heard herself say as if she was deep underwater.

"Yes," was all Jess said.

❧❧❧❧

Twenty-four hours later, here they were in this little cabin. Instead of cooking dinner, Casey spent most of her time staring at Jess in the shower and as a result, dinner took much longer than anticipated. When Jess came out of the bedroom wearing black yoga pants and a white tank top, her wet blond hair leaving trails of water down her neck, Casey felt her breath catch in her throat. Usually Casey was an excellent cook, but with Jess so close, watching her, she became flustered. She's pretty sure Jess caught onto that.

Jess hopped up on the kitchen counter, her athletic legs dangling off the side. Casey handed Jess a glass of white wine and tried to re-focus on dinner, but all she could imagine was leaning in between Jess's legs as she wrapped her arms sand legs around her.

"What are we having for dinner?" Asked Jess innocently, shocking Casey out of her little daydream.

"Sautéed chicken, veggies and couscous, if that's okay."

"Sound delish. I'm just going to put on some more

music."

"My phone is right there," Casey responded, her legs wobbling a little bit.

Jess (of course) picked a play list of Casey's entitled "Thinking of Her." Casey finished preparing dinner and set the small kitchen table. As they sat on opposite ends of the table listening to love song after love song, Casey wondered if Jess knew those songs were meant for her.

After an awkward dinner of not much conversation, Jess suggested they sit outside by the fire pit. "Do you have another sweatshirt? I forgot mine," said Jess.

"Sure. It's in the dresser in the bedroom. Be warned though, it's my favorite."

A few moments later, Jess came out wearing Casey's favorite Skidmore sweatshirt. She went outside to prepare the fire pit while Casey cleaned up the kitchen. She pulled the Adirondack chairs near the fire pit and moved the Bluetooth speaker outside so they could listen to music by the fire.

After a few failed tries, they finally got the fire blazing. It was a beautiful clear and cool night, and the stars were out in force. Casey's contribution was a bottle of Patron tequila. Casey knew if she drank too much, her abilities to hold her feelings back from Jess might be compromised.

Jess's head was tipped back on the Adirondack chair, her legs curled tightly in against her. They took turns taking small swigs directly from the ice cold bottle.

Her voice broke the silence. "You know, I've never seen a shooting star."

"Ahh, those are rare and beautiful moments." Casey said wistfully. "Everyone should see at least one shooting star. It helps us remember that there's still some mystery left. At least that's what my Dad always said."

They stared up at the sky, and Casey silently hoped Jess would see her first shooting star on this night, with her. After Casey saw two more, Jess jumped up and yelled, "Hey! I saw one!"

Taking her hand, Casey said, "See, I knew you would." They remained like that for a moment, holding hands before Casey broke free and turned her face away from Jess.

"What's wrong?" Jess asked.

"Nothing. Nothing's wrong," Casey replied a little too curtly. "I'm fine. It's the tequila."

"No it's not. It's something else," she said.

"I'm used to being alone now, I wasn't ready for this—feeling like this with you," Casey said honestly.

"Casey, I feel the same way. I wasn't exactly looking for anyone and then there you were standing in front of me and I haven't been able to stop thinking about you ever since," responded Jess. "Wait, I want to play a song for you." Jess picked up Casey's cell phone off the Adirondack chair. Moments later, Sade's *By Your Side* bounced off all the trees around them. Sade's smooth voice sang, "You think I'd leave your side baby, you know me better than that. Think I'd leave you down when you're down on your knees, I wouldn't do that... If only you could see into me..."

Jess sat back down facing Casey, looking into her eyes. Jess just looked at Casey while the song played, without saying a word. The fire cracked and hissed. Jess and the crickets, and the breeze and Sade. Casey didn't move, and wondered if Jess was trying to decide what to do next. Or maybe it was Casey trying to decide what to do next.   As if reading her mind, Jess said barely loud enough for Casey to hear, "You're not alone, Casey.

Not anymore."

Before Casey had a chance to respond, Jess stood up and took Casey's hand, leading her into the house.

The cabin door slammed behind them and Casey could feel her heart beat in her mouth. Jess led Casey to the bedroom and lit a few candles. Sade echoed through the trees and the open window. Casey sat down on the bed and Jess stood in front of her letting Casey straddle her. Jess touched Casey's face gently with her palm and leaned down to kiss her. It was so soft, so warm, so unexpected. Instinct took over. Casey's hands were on her back, pulling Jess toward her. Her lips were amazing. This kiss was amazing. Casey felt Jess's tongue in her mouth and then she was completely on fire. Casey pulled Jess down on her and could feel her weight against her own body. Casey's hands ran down Jess's back and up to her neck. She had an amazing body, and Casey wanted to touch all of it. She gently pulled off her Skidmore sweatshirt that now was in an entirely new category of favorite, then her tank top. Casey looked at Jess's gorgeously strong body and had a new appreciation for dancers. Jess tugged at Casey's sweatshirt, then at her jeans. Casey pulled off her own sweatshirt and jeans in a matter of seconds.

Casey rolled Jess over on her stomach and moved down her back with her tongue. Jess smelled like vanilla and tasted even better. When Casey's lips reached her lower back, Jess arched up to meet her and Casey thought she would explode. Jess turned over, her hips rising up to meet Casey's mouth. Casey lowered her mouth on her slowly, opening Jess up with her tongue. Jess was so hot and so wet. Casey found her clit and began massaging it slowly with her tongue. With every flick she could feel her body jolt, a small electric current running through her. Casey did this until she heard Jess say her name over and over again, "Casey, Casey, please." Then Casey plunged her tongue deeper and deeper into her. Jess's hips rocked against Casey, their hands were locked together. Jess's orgasm came quickly, but Casey continued to touch her, knowing that was just the beginning. She replaced her tongue with fingers and Jess moaned. Casey moved slowly at first, until she could feel Jess's muscles tighten around her hand. Casey pressed her body against Jess and kissed her hard. Jess's blue eyes remained open the entire time, and they stared at each other while Jess came and Casey came, over and over again.

Jess sat up, and Casey with her so that her legs were over Casey's. They faced each other. Jess ran her fingers ran through Casey's long black hair, which reached just below Casey's shoulders.

"I love your hair," Jess said. "I've imagined how soft it would be. And your eyes, are they grey or charcoal?" Before Casey could answer, Jess kissed Casey again, this time deeper than Casey had ever been kissed before. Jess's hands were moving from Casey's breasts down her side and up her back. Casey had no idea where they were going next and didn't care so long as they continued to touch her.

If Jess continued to kiss Casey that way, Casey was going to have an orgasm right there, but Jess's right hand had another idea. She held Casey's back with her left hand while her right dipped between Casey's legs. She found her clit in, oh, about a second and began rubbing it with her thumb. Casey moaned into her mouth as Jess kept kissing her, her tongue tracing Casey's lips and then plunging deeper and deeper into her mouth. Casey bit Jess's lip when she entered her.

Jess's thumb stayed on Casey's clit and her fingers, maybe her hand, maybe her entire arm, entered Casey. Jess's rhythm was slow and steady. Casey arched her head back, breaking their kiss for the first time. Jess's lips just found their way to Casey's neck. She continued her steady movement and Casey held on for dear life. Casey thought she saw shooting stars, or at least that's how she wanted to remember it.

"Come with me," Jess said, rising from the bed a few minutes after Casey had come back down to earth.

"Are you sure we can walk?" Casey protested.

Jess led them to the shower room and turned on the faux waterfall.

"Do you know why we're in here?"

"Because you needed to cool off?" Casey laughed, nuzzling her lips into Jess's neck.

"No. Because I wanted to do this to you today when we were at the creek. You knew that, right?"

Before Casey had a chance to reply, Jess held her shoulders and gently pushed her back against the waterfall. As the hot water rushed over their heads, Jess kissed Casey again, pulling her close until they both knew for certain this was the one singularly perfect love they had both been waiting for.

Lucy J. Madison is an author, screenwriter, and poet. Her work often delves into the intricacies of relationships, passion, and love. She resides with her wife of sixteen years in Connecticut and in Provincetown, MA along with their beloved pets.

Website: www.lucyjmadison.com